Bonito Deputy

Pacifying the wild streets of Bonito would have been a challenge for any man, but when the lawman chosen to undertake the task was yet to turn twenty-one, the inhabitants of the hell-town had good reason to be afraid.

Rick Dannecker knew what the townsfolk were thinking . . . but he also knew that the man brave enough to take on the impossible could see his name become legend. . . .

Bonito Deputy

Jack Slade

ROBERT HALE · LONDON

First published in Great Britain 2010

ISBN 978-0-7090-8975-9

Robert Hale Limited
Clerkenwell House
Clerkenwell Green
London EC1R 0HT

www.halebooks.com

Typeset by
Derek Doyle & Associates, Shaw Heath
Printed and bound in Great Britain by
CPI Antony Rowe, Chippenham and Eastbourne

CHAPTER 1

SHOWDOWN

Patrolling Bonito any Saturday night was more than a job for just one man and Deputy Jack Hart knew this better than anybody. Still, that was just what he did each and every Saturday, walked these streets alone after Deputy Hogue Harvey had been shot dead a month back leaving just himself and second-deputy Rick Dannecker to carry on. Hart did not look upon himself as any kind of hero, but if the wild men wanted a tin star to aim at when they got to raising hell he would much rather it be his than the boy's . . . as would any man worth his salt, or so he believed.

It had turned chilly with the sun gone down but

some quality in the air did not hold the dust, so that the air of Main Street was clear and strangely sweet as Deputy Jack Hart made his way back from supper at the New York Café. Men lounged in groups along the plankwalk of the central block, leaning lazily against store-fronts or seated upon the tie-rail where a number of horses were hitched. They talked in low voices and here and there among them was the orange glow of a cheroot or the quick flare of a match flame. They fell silent as the lawman passed. They were cowboys. In the silence as the badgeman passed on by, there was only the creaking of the tie-rail, the hollow clump of one man's boot-heels to be heard.

He walked on through the thin stripes of light thrown out by the louvres of the High Pocket Saloon. One by one other groups fell quiet before him here – and these were not all cowhands. He felt a familiar tightening of his stomach muscles as faces averted from his flat stare. He figured he knew why they reacted that way. It was on account they were figuring him dead already and found themselves unable to meet the eye of a corpse.

He smiled crookedly and glanced down proudly at the little point of light shimmering off the star pinned to his vest.

It was still quiet enough, he told himself, for a Saturday night. But it would not stay that way. Not with the hands from the Running S taking on liquid freight heavily at the Cage, and the crews from the Clover Leaf and Lazy Y downing double brandies at the High Pocket it would not.

He continued onwards neither quick nor slow, a gloomy-featured and narrow-waisted lawman with a limp that was a legacy of a gunfight right here on the streets of Bonito several years before.

First Deputy Jack Hart was the last of the old-time lawmen of Bonito, now that Hogue Harvey was dead and gone.

During the regime he'd shared with Harvey they had maintained a tolerably high level of law enforcement in this turbulent town. Mostly, it was the rough-and-ready brand of law of the gunbarrel and ready-boot variety, but it had worked most always.

Hart was a decent and honourable man. He had coped with problems night and day – with brawling, drunken miners, as well as the cowboys who had a special weakness for riding horses into crowded saloons, hotels or billiard parlours, who loved nothing better than to shoot the chimneys out of the chandeliers.

The position of deputy of Bonito was a

dangerous and at times fatal one, and members of the Citizens' Committee often puzzled that there was mostly someone ready to take on the job after some unlucky tinstar either quit and ran or was gunned down.

But now they were worried as was the deputy himself. For should anything befall him there was no street-wise old badge-toter to step into his boots, only a nineteen-year old youth just one month in the job.

True, that boy was the son of Lige Dannecker, now old and crippled, but once the town's most illustrious citizen and formidable first-deputy.

But good blood lines didn't make up for youth and inexperience – or so the lawman told himself as he passed by the Glenn Horn Hotel.

It was the cowboys who were the main trouble, of course. The men from the giant spreads such as Clover Leaf and the Lazy Y, but most of all those riders from the Running S. That outfit was the largest and the worst, mainly because Buck Silver, who had recently inherited the spread from his father, was more of a hell-raiser than most wild men on his payroll, and the cowboys simply took their cue from him.

The peace officer finally stopped off for a mug of coffee after his first full patrol of Apache Street, at the Green Dollar Café. Owner Jennings was gabby as usual, but the lawman only managed grunts by way of response.

'Big night brewing, Deputy?'

'Could be.'

'Hands in from Clover Leaf and Lazy Y, too.'

'Do tell.'

Jennings studied his customer more closely now. 'You look a little peaked, Deputy. I always say your job is way too much for one man . . . wouldn't you agree?'

Hart lowered his mug. 'That'd depend on the man, I reckon, Jennings.'

The man straightened and flushed a little. 'Heck, never meant to offend you none, Deputy, just makin' small talk. Er, 'scuse me, couple of customers just arrived.'

Hart stared moodily into the mug cupped between his thick-knuckled hands. It wasn't his nature to be terse, it was just those damned cowhands. Hell-raising and carrying on the way they did, they were always itching for trouble, seemed to him.

Abruptly, he spun a coin on to the table and quit the eatery.

It was dark when he emerged into lamplit Apache Street. Two cowboys galloped past scattering folks on the street and yelling like wild Indians.

Jack Hart spat in disgust.

Cowboys!

There was no agreement on this breed in Bonito for however men were hurt, driven out or even killed by the wild men when they liquored up and went loco, there was always their small yet voluble army of defenders ready to rush to their aid whenever they landed in trouble.

Their army of defenders would reason that the cowboys never stuck up banks or robbed stages. Yet by far their most attractive feature – at least in the eyes of saloonkeepers, merchants and gamblers – was the reckless way they hurled their money around, especially when too tanked to know what they were doing.

The deputy had made several serious efforts to clamp down on the wild ones and limit their mischief, but not any longer. The businessmen and saloon bosses and even the sweet ladies who operated the bordellos on Back Street all insisted the cowboys should be allowed their 'little bit of fun', and so nothing was ever done.

But he still had his job to do, and promptly sent two drunken waddies on their way from out front of the funeral parlour. The pair scowled but obeyed sulkily. Men from the Clover Leaf, they were. And further along Apache Street he intervened in a brawl between a half-Mex waddy and Tom Frane, a freighter of the town.

'You OK, Tom?' he asked quietly after the hellion had jumped on his half-wild pony and stormed off down the street at full gallop.

'Yeah, guess so. Damn them – they oughta be behind bars. Seems to me Buck Silver on the Running S is gettin' less and less careful about the hands he signs on these days.'

Deputy Hart stared off along the street, stroking his drooping moustache. He shared the other's opinion of the trouble-makers to a degree, was uneasy about that wild-eyed half-breed with the arrogant walk who seemed to be even more and more on his streets these days. But he dismissed him from his mind. 'Better make for home, Tom,' he advised. 'Could be this night might get worse before it gets better.'

After the man had left, Hart made his way to the Cage where the gambling layouts were in full swing. Whiskey was king at the long, pannelled bar and silver dollars were changing hands fast when he took a final glance around before moving on.

Next stops were the Wayfarer and the Hasta, both doing boom business and each threatening maybe to boil over before the night was through. A warning word here, a wagging finger there and he was on his way and making for the batwings of the High Pocket when the brawl erupted some place in back of him.

'From the Lazy Y!' somebody bawled above the clamour. 'One of 'em lost at cards and pulled a knife.'

He proved able to settle that one down, marched a couple of drunken Running S cowboys off the premises, issued the standard litany of warnings, then hit Main Street again beneath a bloated summer moon.

The whole town was humming by this and he was just congratulating himself for having put the lid on the High Pocket when he heard the sure sounds of further violence drifting from an alley – thuds and curses, the scuffle of high heeled boots.

The star on his vest glinted dully as he stepped into the gloom. 'All right, break it up. What the hell is going on in here?'

The scuffling ceased and three shadowy faces turned towards him. One was a stranger, another a man named O'Malley and the third was the same half-breed wrangler he'd warned off earlier for fighting with Tom Frane – Kip Darby.

'By glory it's good to see you, Deputy,' O'Malley

gasped. The man was bleeding and his shirt was torn. He jerked a thumb at the half-breed. 'He jumped me and I—'

'OK, OK,' the lawman grunted. 'You two, head off home, I'll take care of this one. Yeah, you, Darby, put your hands behind your back. I'm taking you in.'

The two wasted no time in scuttling off, while the barrel-chested half-breed with the flashing black eyes just stood immobile, chin up, chest heaving from exertion.

'I said—' the lawman began but got no further as the half-breed threateningly slapped the handle of the six-gun riding his hip.

'If you got half a brain you'll turn the hell around and get gone, tinstar. You've been pushin' me around since the day I came . . . but you picked the wrong place and the wrong time here. Get gone while you're still able.'

No peace officer could take that. Hart moved another step closer and snapped his fingers. 'The gun . . . now!'

After what seemed a long moment the half-breed shrugged and took out his weapon while holding the trigger-guard with his index finger. Hart half-smiled at the ease of his victory. Next moment he caught the sudden glitter in the brawler's eyes and saw lips curling back from clenched teeth. The six-shooter spun, transcribing a brief blue circle in the half-light and then levelled the instant before boreflame and thunder spewed from the muzzle and the deputy went staggering backwards as his whole world exploded.

The last sensation in his life was the feel of the dust of Apache Street against his face.

Instantly the cowboys whirled about and came rushing back. Benny stood staring down at the lifeless shape while the echoes of the single gunshot still slammed from wall to wall like the hammers of hell.

'You fool!' the cowboy blurted out at length. 'What the hell did you go and do that for? He would have only run you in for the night.'

'He was pushin' me. I don't like to be pushed.'

'Judas Priest – Silver will go loco about this!' the second waddy choked.

The half-breed calmly fingered fresh shells into his Colt. 'What makes him happy don't bother me one lick.' He moved to the alley mouth and looked out to see men boiling out of two saloons close by. 'But maybe we should mosey, boys . . . these drunks might get their tails in a crack over this.' He indicated the lifeless figure of the deputy with the revolver.

'Not that I can figure why. Who really cares about one deputy more or less?'

They stared at him like he was loco. Maybe he was. But they didn't dally, instead took off together following the dark end out then sprinting for the hitchrack out front of the Blue Diamond Saloon.

Swinging up they put spurs to horse-hide to go storming away into the welcoming darkness of the west trail. All three were long gone from sight by the time the first horrified citizen came upon the lifeless form back in the alley and realized what had occurred.

'Get the doc!' the man howled, even though a blind man could see Jack Hart was beyond any help.

Not right away perhaps, but soon enough, this man like every other citizen of Bonito would realize that with their deputy dead, their sole bulwark between themselves and total lawlessness now was a nineteen-year-old boy who had only worn the deputy's star over one brief month.

CHAPTER 2

DRUMS FOR A DEAD DEPUTY

Originally the funeral cortège of any Bonito citizen was accompanied by a full band of trumpets, trombones, a kettle drum and three men playing fiddles.

But that was many years ago now. One by one, the original musicians had passed on, with the newcomers of the expanding West far too preoccupied with making money and carving out their land grabs to bother with mastering musical instruments.

Now all that remained of those originals was a

handful of old greybeards who hopped and propped along side-by-side with the funeral procession to the beat of kettle drums rattling out the last miles for the slain sheriff of Bonito.

It was one of the best-attended burials in the town's history due to the fact that just about every man and woman there wanted to show their respect for a good man who had died defending their freedom and liberty.

Vale Jack Hart!

Second Deputy Rick Dannecker heard the throb of the drums in the jailhouse where he fought the urge to throw the doors open and stand there on the stoop where all could see him while he publicly paid his respects at the final journey of Deputy Jack Hart.

But that would serve no real purpose, he knew, would change nothing. In the thirty-six hours since the deputy had been gunned down he had come to understand completely where he himself stood in the eyes and estimation of the town.

As second deputy to the crusty Hart he had been patronized, flattered, treated as a pleasant young man, tolerated. But since the killing they had shown in no uncertain terms that he was not to be taken seriously as far as assuming authority was concerned.

For he was little more than a boy – right?

Sure, he was Lige Dannecker's son. But a man needed more than simple blood lines to qualify him to stand up before the wild cowboys from the Running S, the Clover Leaf and the Lazy Y. That surely was the task for a man!

Yet despite his youth, he had already displayed a sureness and balance of a man much older. Well-built and athletic with strong shoulders and slim hips, he was handsome with sky-blue eyes and a ready grin that reminded folks of his father at a similar age.

Right at that moment his chin was jutting defiantly and the blue eyes appeared rebellious. For no matter what learned greybeards of the Citizens' Committee might believe to the contrary, the deputy knew he was the man to fill Jack Hart's big boots.

OK, so he was not yet twenty. It was true also he had worn the badge but for one short month before his superior's untimely death. But he had been tried and tested on several occasions and found to be not lacking in either courage or ability. But perhaps most importantly of all, he believed in the law, believed passionately in its wisdom and power.

He shrugged and resumed his restless pacing

across the stone-walled office.

The mute and evil faces of brutal men stared unblinkingly down upon him from the walls – the mocking rogue's gallery of outlaw kings.

And well they might smirk, he mused in a rare moment of self-doubt. For though murder had been done right here in Bonito they had restrained him from making any attempt to identify and deal with those responsible for the crime.

Not that there was much real doubt about who had been responsible, he brooded. But proving it would surely be something else, maybe an impossible challenge.

If one of Buck Silver's riders had murdered the marshal, how would he get to prove it? And how would Buck take it should he try? For Buck was a big man, hard, arrogant and a law to himself – everyone knew that.

No, they didn't have to tell him this any more than they needed to point out that the deputy was dead and gone and that no amount of investigating or suspicion would bring him back. So they might as well let it drop – right?

He shook his head. No. Wrong. That might be the way of others; it was not his.

Deep in thought he didn't hear the door opening above the sound of the drums – didn't lift his eyes from the floor until a light voice said, 'May I come in?'

He looked up to see Judy Stanley standing in the doorway. She looked just as pert and pretty as always, and seeing her now like this was doubly pleasurable, considering his heavy mood. He crossed swiftly to her and closed the door behind her to muffle once again the sounds of the cortège which had almost passed on by.

'Judy. I didn't figure on seeing you today. Better take a seat.'

She smiled as he held a chair out for her. 'Just for a minute, Rick.' She waited while he dusted off the chair with a bandanna. Seating herself gracefully, she removed her white gloves and glanced around. She looked out at the passageway leading through to the cells and waved at a bearded, red-eyed face squinting out through the bars. 'Hello, Arch!'

'Hi there, Miss Judy!'

Rick grinned for maybe the first time in the past thirty-six hours. Then he was sober again. 'You not going on to the cemetery, Judy?'

She shook her head. 'Father and mother are attending. I didn't wish to go because funerals depress me so. But I imagined you would be there, Rick?'

He toyed with the inkstand and leaned a hip against the desk. 'No. Jack knew I liked him. Buryings depress me like they do you.'

'That's not the real reason, is it, Rick?'

He studied her closely. 'What do you mean?'

'You are angry because they haven't made you first deputy, aren't you?'

'Who put that into your head? Your father, was it?'

'Well, yes, as a matter of fact it was.' She paused, serious-faced. She was a slender, supple-bodied girl with grey eyes that shone like sunlight on raindrops. 'But I knew how you would feel without being told by anyone.'

'It's a pity your father didn't pay more attention to putting some real stiffening into the Citizens' Committee instead of griping about how inexperienced I am and the rest. You ought to ask him if he ever heard of Billy the Kid sometime. Ask him if they made him show his birth certificate before he let daylight into all those poor jaspers he killed down south.'

'Good heavens! Surely you aren't comparing yourself to that horrible little butcher are you, Rick?'

He thrust both hands deep in his pockets and leaned against the door frame. 'Ah . . . you know

I'm not doing that, Judy. It's just that I'm so damned angry at the way they're all tucking their heads under because they're afraid.'

'Does that mean you think Father is also afraid?'

'I don't know if he is or not,' he said bluntly.

'Well—'

'Now, don't get riled. He's no better or worse than anyone else. But as chairman of the Citizens' Committee I'd surely like to see him take a stronger stand. . . .'

'I see.'

'No, you don't!'

She studied him carefully for a long moment in silence. She knew how strong he already was, how quickly he was developing now. This both impressed and frightened her. She would not admit even to herself that she found his strength so magnetic and attractive mainly because it contrasted so sharply with the weakness she knew to be in her father.

Whenever Rick Dannecker got that glitter in his eye she knew it was time to step lightly, yet there was more at stake here than sparing his feelings.

'Father honestly believes you are too young for the responsibility that comes with the office of first deputy, Rick.'

He made an impatient gesture as he went to the

door and swung it open. The street lay empty before him. The funeral procession of Jack Hart had disappeared from sight around the corner of the New York Café.

'I know what they think. But they're wrong. I can handle this job as well or better than anyone I know.'

She smiled to herself at this unconscious egotism. Rising from the desk, she joined him in the wide stone doorway. 'Nobody wants to see you throw your life away, Rick.'

'Are you playing the same tune as everyone else now, Judy?'

'Don't be foolish, honey. It's just that – well, I do believe you should have more time to adjust to the new work and responsibility. So, don't be cross with me. I'm on your side, remember?'

Somehow he managed a tight grin. 'Sure . . . I remember.'

As they stood side by side in awkward silence for a time, Rick felt he wanted to talk but seemed unable to get the injustice of Hart's death from his mind. The distant rattle of kettle drums only seemed to deepen his mood, while the girl made a little ceremony of drawing on her white kid gloves.

Then she said, 'What will they do now, Rick?

The Committee, I mean.'

'You mean about filling the post of first deputy?'

'Yes.'

'Send out of town, maybe to Oxbend. The way things are breaking here with the hands from the big spreads riding wild and roughshod, they're going to need some pretty fancy badgetoter to reign them in. Could be they'll pick up some big-name gunslinger at top dollar and pin a badge on him. That's happened in plenty towns since cattle got to be so big.'

'What about Sheriff Gammel? He must approve any applicant and we all know how he feels about gunfighters and such.'

'Yeah, we all sure know that.'

Sheriff Ryle Gammel was sheriff of the neighbouring town of Oxbend, the county seat. He was also administrator of the county and, despite repeated petitions and pleas, had refused to grant Bonito full charter.

Some believed this stemmed from jealousy, as Bonito now rivalled Oxbend in size and importance and was freely tipped to overtake it within the next year. Meantime Bonito civic leaders had to be content with living directly under the authority of the Oxbend sheriff, and rumour had it that his decisions had more to do with the condition of his liver at any given time than following the letter of the law.

He glanced sideways at the girl, read her expression. He nodded and kept his tone casual as he said, 'Well, what is it?'

She feigned innocence. 'What is what?'

'Whatever it is that's on your mind and you're trying to keep secret from me, of course,' he half-smiled.

She sobered. 'Well, I'll only consider telling you because I understand how you feel about your half-brother, Rick—'

'Quint? Something about Quint? What?'

'Now, please calm down. I don't even know if they were serious, but I heard Father say that if there was one man who could likely put a stop to the violence that threatens to destroy our town, it would have to be Quint Dannecker.'

'They're going to invite Quint back here?' He could barely contain his excitement.

'I think they mean to raise it at the next meeting of the Committee that's tomorrow night. Oh, Rick, I do hope he comes, for your sake. And for mine too, of course You've told me so much about him he sounds like a combination of Galahad and George Washington.'

He grinned, at last putting the grim scene being

enacted out at the cemetery from his mind. It was years since he'd seen his famous half-brother during which time Quint's deeds had so built him up in Rick's mind that he'd come to look upon him as some kind of living legend. It was hard to believe he might be showing up here – just when he might be needed most.

Judy smiled understandingly.

'Now, Rick, all I said was that they were discussing the possibility. I certainly know there are other candidates for the post of first deputy here.'

'Nobody would out-rank Quint – not if they really want the best.'

'Perhaps that is so. But if they should make that decision, then what of Sheriff Gammel?'

He frowned, then shrugged. 'The committee will take care of Gammell – if they really want him. Say, I wonder if Dad's heard about all this? He'd be downright proud if it went ahead. Can you imagine it, Judy? Dad and Quint and me all together in the same town again after all this time. I never thought I'd live to see the day.'

She placed a hand on his arm.

'Don't tell him yet, Rick. It hasn't happened yet. But I hope it will, for your sake.'

She turned to survey the street.

'Well, I'd best be getting back to the house before Mother and Father return. 'Bye for now, Rick.'

'So long Judy . . . and thanks.'

He watched her out of sight then remained in the doorway overlooking the street, his mind filled with images of his brother – vivid pictures of an heroic, larger-than-life figure that had filled his imagination for as long as he could remember.

He was still there, dragging on a cigarette, when the mourners began returning from the graveyard. They came by carthorse, buggy, buckboard and on foot. He realized that most of the town had gone out to hear the last words for Jack Hart – last of the old-time lawmen.

Many nodded sympathetically across at the youthful deputy, all of them aware of the strong comradeship that had existed between him and Hart. He returned their greetings solemnly. The town's dignitaries were last to appear, led by the tall, immaculate figure of Chad Stanley, Judy's father. But his gaze tightened as he identified Stanley's companion, a tall and wide-shouldered figure in expensively tailored black broadcloth: Buck Silver.

Rick stepped back inside the door before the

group passed by. He wasn't about to exchange greetings with Silver, not today of all days. Few men would have the gall to attend the funeral of a respected peace officer, gunned down as everyone suspected, by one of Silver's own men.

But this display was only too typical of Silver, Rick brooded, totally in keeping with his arrogance.

Rick's cold stare drilled at the tall figure as he rode past on his big sorrel, chatting to Stanley who at least was sufficiently moved by the ceremony he'd just witnessed to wear a solemn face. Nonetheless, the banker *was* accompanying Silver, thus showing the town he did not believe he'd had anything to do with the killing.

Rick ground his teeth.

A scene such as this would never be repeated once Quint got to wear the star here, so he believed. In his mind he already had his brother walking the streets and alleys of Bonito. It never entered his mind that Quint might not even be traceable, or that he might reject the town's offer. It was even possible that the committee might reject his nomination for one of many other reasons.

For in his mind, it was already set in stone: Quint would be first deputy with himself as his *segundo.* The town of Bonito would be troubled no longer, tamed and secure by the best kind of law – Dannecker law.

CHAPTER 3

VOTE FOR A FAST GUN

The Bonito Citizens' Committee met in the courthouse at eight the night following the burial of First Deputy Jack Hart.

Such meetings where the policies of Bonito were formulated were usually serious affairs, but the face of each man as he entered the chamber tonight was downright solemn. For not only had a respected citizen been slain but their town was now without a recognized peace officer.

One by one they removed their headgear and took their places around the long oak table. There was Varn Tidrick of Tidrick's Store, Rob Ramsey of the Bonito Fast Freight, Rolfe from the New York Café and Lige Dannecker of Dannecker's Saddlers arriving with Jake Prescott of the general store.

Dannecker was last to take his place, encumbered as he was by his wheelchair. Rob Ramsey drew two chairs away to make space for him at the head of the table. When all was quiet, President Chad Stanley called upon Secretary Harry Rolfe to read the minutes of the previous meeting, which had been held in circumstances far different from the present.

The original organization from which the Citizens' Committe sprang was actually known as the Bonito Merchants' Association. Its task was to nourish all types of commercial enterprise in the town and act as a united voice when such matters as freight charges and protection of local produce arose.

Over time, the canny merchants and citizens had weeded out the cattlemen from the original association, for by then cattle were booming and the locals feared to give the ranchers more power than they would naturally acquire through growing wealth. Such people as saloon owners, gambling halls and sporting houses were summarily cast out also on the grounds that their interests were not in the best interests of the town.

The committee thus had been whittled down to the 'right-thinking' people – the better class of citizen. Purified and regimented they had become the Citizens' Committee of Bonito.

They still campaigned actively for a town patent, sending regular delegations to Oxbend with petitions and arguments, but in the interim they enforced the law to the best of their ability.

Secretary Rolfe concluded the reading of the minutes, then sat down abruptly on realizing nobody was really paying any attention. With customary dignity, President Stanley rose from his seat at the head of the table.

'Comments upon the minutes?' he asked, knowing there would be none. Heads shook in unison. He hooked thumbs in the armholes of his sober vest and leaned back on his heels. 'Gentlemen, there is no need to remind you all that this meeting has been convened at a time of crisis – a time when a loyal and courageous employee of this very committee has been feloniously slain and so leaves us with no suitable man to take his place.'

'Might I have a word, Chad?' said Lige Dannecker. He was a powerful, grey-haired citizen with a formidable presence, despite his handicap.

'Of course, Lige, though I have a feeling I know what you're going to say.'

'If you think I'm fixin' to ask why you don't make my boy Rick first deputy, then you're right.'

A murmur rippled around the big table. Stanley silenced it with a curt gesture. 'Lige,' he said, 'Rick is simply too young. We're not casting any reflections on the boy, but you saw yourself what can happen even to an experienced man like Jack Hart. Think what might happen to a youth not quite twenty who has only worn the star for one short month.'

'He's as much a man as any I know twice his age,' Dannecker senior defended stubbornly.

'He might well be at that, Lige,' put in Rob Ramsey. 'But that is a risk we can't take – neither with his life nor our own safety.'

'I tell you he can handle the job,' Dannecker insisted. 'I know the boy's capabilities and I'm here to tell you all that he'd most likely make the best deputy Bonito's ever seen.'

'Now come on, Lige,' Stanley protested. 'You can't really believe that. This town has had a distinguished line of deputies, including yourself. We can't expect young Rick to measure up to those standards. Later, when he's put on a few years and pounds, perhaps, but not yet.'

'I still says he's the man for the job.'

'Lige,' Stanley sighed, 'do you want me to put it to the vote?'

Dannecker glanced around at the stern faces. He didn't need to call for a count or show of hands to know where he stood.

'No,' he finally rumbled, 'I guess not.'

'Now don't be disappointed, Lige,' the president said. He glanced around conspiratorilly at the other members before coming back to Dannecker. 'You see, Lige, we already plan to nominate your son as First Deputy of Bonito.'

Dannecker blinked. 'My son? But you just said that—'

'Not Rick, Lige – Quint!'

'Quint!'

'I discussed it with the other members in private before we assembled, Lige. Like myself they feel we need a genuine gunfighter and hard man as law here in Bonito these rough times – one who can match those gun-happy hooligans at their own game.'

'But Quint. . . ?' Dannecker was obviously stunned by this turn of events. 'Why him?'

'Why not – I believe would be a far better question, Lige,' Stanley countered. 'All of us remember Quint Dannecker from an earlier time when he was – to put it mildly – quite a wild boy. But that was nine years ago. A man matures in that time. We've all read how Quint has had gunfights in various places and has never been defeated. He grew up here in this town, was always a natural leader. And none of us have forgotten the splendid services rendered to this town by his father and our fellow committeeman – your own good self!'

Applause rattled around the table, but died away as they realized Lige himself seemed anything but approving of their proposal. Stanley again achieved silence before speaking up again.

'What is it, Lige? We thought the news would delight you. Don't you think Quint would ideally fill the shoes of first deputy?'

There was silence.

'Only what, Lige?'

But Lige Dannecker remained silent. He loved his oldest son and could not find it within himself to express his fear that Quint – handsome, dashing and deadly Quint – might cause more trouble than he could prevent.

Which meant that when the vote was called for it was unanimously in favour of inviting Quint Dannecker to become first deputy of Bonito.

*

Blood trickled from the cowboy's top lip as he shook his head and struggled to rise from the saloon floor. He would have succeeded but for the kick Coulter caught him with that rolled him across the bar room floor, where he cannoned into Jack Murtz.

'That tears it,' growled the husky Murtz, and leaping the prone figure, he dropped his head and charged.

'Judas Priest!' gasped the barkeep of the Days of Glory Saloon, and rushed to protect his bottled supplies. For this was where the wild ones of the county tended to gather, and wherever they assembled these days there were brawls just like this one.

A ragged cheer rose when Murtz's charge came to nothing as a woolly-headed cowhand from the Cross 20 stuck out a boot to trip him up . . . and the full-blooded brawl that flowed from there soon had barkeep Willy Hayes grabbing down his bottled stock from the shelves and moaning to anyone that wanted to listen, 'By God and by Judas – those stuffed shirts at the committee meetin' had better find someone who can keep this fool town peaceful otherwise there ain't gonna be no town come fall!'

Nobody challenged what might have sounded

like a gross exaggeration to any newcomer to Bonito. The committee just had to come up with some badgeman capable of enforcing law and order. But where would you find such a rare species? Maybe they didn't exist any longer?

'Well, Lige?' the chairman said testily as the silence dragged on. 'Have you got some suggestion to make about appointing Quint, or ain't you?'

Lige Dannecker looked up, realized the entire meeting was waiting on him to answer what Stanley had been saying.

He stared at the window. From somewhere downtown came the crash of breaking furniture, a familiar sound in town these days.

He straightened and folded his arms. 'Well, on account I might know my first-born better than most of you, my first thought about offering him any kind of peace-keeping job could be like asking a fire-bug to run the fire station. Anyone agree with that?'

Several heads nodded. It might well be a long time since Quint Dannecker had raised hell on the streets of town, but those who dated back to that time remembered it well enough.

'But, Lige,' said Harry Rolfe, 'that was years

back. He'd be a mature man by this, would have to have quietened down plenty by now.'

'Only wish I could be as sure of that as you seem to be,' Dannecker replied.

'Well,' the chairman sighed, 'guess you'd be a better judge on that than any of us. But, dang it, this still sounds like a good notion to me. I mean, your boy knows the town, he's a natural take-charge kind of feller ... you heard from him lately, Lige?'

'Not lately.' Dannecker gazed at the windows. 'He's written me about once a year since he left town – sometimes for money, but not always, and not for quite a time recent. Far as I can make out he's tackled just about every job under the sun – shotgun guard on payroll coaches, not to mention mining and prospecting. And, of course, getting into gunfights and brawls, mostly over women, from what I can make out.'

Chad Stanley lowered himself into his leather chair. He was sober as he studied the faces of his fellow-councillors before turning back to Lige.

'Well, you claim you're not against our proposal out-of-hand, Lige, but you sure sound like you're trying to turn us off the notion of maybe contacting your boy and getting him to pin on the badge.'

Stanley waited for a response but there was none. He drew a cheroot from a vest pocket and toyed with it as he studied the one-time lawman.

'The way I see it, Lige, you've not told us anything we don't know. So Quint was a wild boy. So what? We've got a whole town full of that breed and we're plumb sick of griping about it and doing nothing. Every man Jack of us knows what Quint was like, and most likely still is. To that I say – who cares? We know him, know what he can do. And we don't want a moral paragon, we want a lawman – a fighter, goddamnit!'

Murmurs of agreement broke out around the table.

'That's it in a nutshell, Lige,' offered Varn Tidrick. 'What we plainly need here in Bonito is a gunfighter . . . not another desk jockey.'

'You're proposing to fight fire with fire,' Dannecker said stubbornly.

'Maybe,' Stanley agreed. 'But we assembled here today to come to a decision. Sure, we don't want to turn our town into another Dodge or Tombstone, which is why we reckon we should go with someone we know and even like to handle the job. That adds up to your boy Quint.'

Mumurs of agreement spread around the table.

'So that's it, plain and simple, Lige,' repeated

Tidrick. 'What we need here in Bonito right now is a gunfighter.'

'There's plenty of that breed about,' Dannecker said harshly.

'We know it,' said Stanley. 'We are looking to your boy, Quint. Nobody else fills the bill.'

Dannecker studied the assembled faces for a long moment, finally sighed and put down his pipe.

'I'm not knocking my own boy even though it might sound like I am. I believe Quint has likely matured and changed, but he's still got that reputation and reputations can always draw trouble. I say I don't believe it's worth that risk.'

'We've already talked it over between us, Lige,' the president replied firmly. 'We shall, of course, give Gammel the opportunity of sanctioning Quint as first deputy. But even if he refuses then we propose to make Quint a special marshal, answerable to us alone.'

Lige wrinkled his forehead. 'Any marshal elected just by us ain't got a legal position as far as the county law's concerned, you know that.'

'Nevertheless, it is legal to elect such a man, providing we don't ask him to interfere in county affairs,' stated Jake Prescott, the committee's expert on legal matters. 'It's been done in other towns. They call it local government by default . . . or by acceptance. That means that citizens of a place without a town patent are legally entitled to take any measures necessary to acquire or defend their security, providing they act at all times within the framework of the law.'

'That might well be legal, Jake, but will it work in practice?' Dannecker asked thoughtfully.

'What about promoting Rick to a higher posting?' someone suggested after a silence.

Stanley shook his head emphatically. 'No. We have no doubt he will rise to first deputy, for the boy has already shown great promise. But we certainly could not burden him with too much responsibility too soon – such a move could surely prove disastrous.'

Dannecker was silent for a time after that, deep in thought. At last he stirred.

'Well, with all that considered, all I can do is throw my weight behind you.' He took a crumpled envelope from his shirt pocket and studied it briefly.

'His address at last writing was the Bonanza Hotel, El Paso, Texas. He wrote this letter to me three months back. He also said he was thinking of heading up towards Austin to handle some horse-breaking there. You'd likely get mail to him at one of those places or the other.'

'You won't regret this, Lige,' Chad Stanley said fruitily. Then, with with the fingers of both smooth hands pressing down upon the table top, he looked from face to face of his committee members. 'Well, gentlemen, I take this opportunity to propose formally that we send for Quint Dannecker, post-haste. All in favour, please raise your right hands.'

The vote was unanimous.

Afterwards, Secretary Harry Rolfe took pen in hand, and, assisted by suggestions from various members, drew up the first rough draft of a letter to Quint Dannecker, late of El Paso, offering him the position of Special Marshal of Bonito at a salary to be determined should he accept the offer. In the end, there was only one man present who didn't believe that they were taking a great step forward towards their goal of making Bonito the peaceful, prosperous town which they all wanted it to become.

But Lige Dannecker was prepared to accept the majority decision.

CHAPTER 4

THE WAITING GAME

The weeks of waiting were beginning to drag for Rick Dannecker the night Toby Willis ran amok.

Toby was large and amiable sober, still large but anything but amiable when drunk .... and this was a miner who dearly loved his liquor,

By the time Rick reached the Three Aces that night a lot of damage had been done, most of it to the saloonkeeper and his bouncers, two of whom were stretched out unconscious upon the bar room floor when Rick arrived after having been awakened from sound sleep by the noise of violence.

He strode through the batwings and propped. Toby had the saloon-keeper by the throat and was bending him backwards over his own bar and threatening the man with a bottle – really threatening and genuinely drunk.

Rick seized the husky brawler, who let go of the saloon-keeper but only in order to let fly with a whistling right hook that might have finished the deputy for the night had it connected.

It didn't connect.

Rick ducked low, felt the rush of displaced air as the big-knuckled fist whistled overhead, then came up and counter-punched.

Toby Willis couldn't believe it. The two had brawled in schooldays and Rick had been laid up for a month as a result.

But in the intervening years Rick had learned how to handle drunks on the streets of Bonito while Toby beat up second-raters and drank more beer than any man in town.

Maybe it was all that beer, Toby thought foggily as he hit the saloon floor and bounced. But he had his pride, and was up in an instant and might have ripped the deputy's head off with that whistling right hook, had it connected.

But it didn't. What connected was the deputy's straight right to the jaw that sent the wild drunk walking backwards halfway across the room before his boot-heel snagged on an uneven floorboard and he fell on his back with a crash heard out at the city limits.

By the time the wild one came to he was wrapped up in a grey jailhouse blanket and blinking at the moon through prison bars. On the other side of the bars, the deputy was dabbing iodine on the knuckle-graze he'd sustained when belting Toby down for the long count.

The brawl was a diversion, but nothing more. Next morning, as usual, saw the deputy jumping from bed to hustle out into the yard looking for any travel-stained horse that might have brought a weary rider in overnight.

None had.

He was aware that this was hardly the way a full-blown deputy sheriff should be carrying on, but it wasn't every day a man's elder brother was heading home after a gap of five years.

He'd often puzzled why Quint had stayed away so long, couldn't figure how he'd apparently never felt moved to come back and at least visit with their father.

The way he figured, Quint lived such a hectic life, by all reports, that he'd have had trouble getting back, even if he'd felt like it.

In the meantime, Rick spied on the old man, knew that he was out in the yard in his wheelchair staring down the road every morning before he himself was properly awake.

Quint Dannecker was a popular subject of discussion all over town during those long, slow weeks of waiting, and the deputy soon realized a lot of that speculation was now being focused upon Buck Silver. Buck and Quint had gone to school together and later had drunk, fought, and rattled Bonito to its foundations with a series of spectacular fights that proved nothing beyond the fact that each man could hold his own and neither had ever seemed to have heard of the word 'quit'.

It was going to be interesting, he'd already heard folks say, how things might evolve here with Quint as marshal and Silver now boss of the Running S.

Just about every visitor to the jailhouse these days only pretended to have some matter on his mind. Callers came to learn the latest on Quint, talk about him and the old times. And not all the visitors were male. The women also came by, most of them now sporting wedding bands, some already mothers but still sparkling-eyed when they asked after his brother and the eternal question,

'When might we expect him, Rick?'

He didn't know. And when he reported these incidents to the old man, Lige would invariably growl, 'Women and guns – guns and women! You'd think your brother was still a schoolboy, the way folks gossip. It's my opinion he'll be a sober, serious lawman by this, doing his job right and likely planning to settle down and wed by about now. Or at least he ought to be.'

'You really believe that, Dad?'

The older man grinned. 'Am I ever wrong?' he joked.

'You were wrong when you said he'd be back years before this.'

And so both men waited. As did the citizens' committee, all the old friends, the still young-and-pretty women from the past, the wild cowboys from the spreads plus the just plain curious. And with the weeks stretching out, it enabled a band of mature ladyfolks to complete an ambitious undertaking, namely, the lettering of a huge calico strip which was strung from the first floor of the Appleseed Hotel all the way across the main street to the flagpole of the courthouse. In two-feet high crimson letters the legend read:

WELCOME HOME QUINT DANNECKER

They planned a real homecoming.

Bonito lay roughly in the centre of some of the best cattle country in the north-west.

Unlike its twin town of Oxbend some thirty miles to the north, which had been born in the gold strikes, Bonito was a cattle town and had always been one.

Lagging somewhat behind the sudden-rich towns like Oxbend and, further afield, Tower and Sam's Landing, Bonito had finally boomed when the great drives to the new railhead began, then gained even greater momentum when the North-Western ran a branch line to its own stockyards there.

All trails, so it appeared, led to Bonito. Now it seemed as if the town had always known the bellowing of cattle and the presence on its streets of lithe, tall cowboys, both from the drives to the shipping yards and from the great spreads which circled the town and from which it derived its wealth.

The trail coming from the south at Sam's Landing had once been part of the main street of a young Bonito. Now it was just another dusty back street that lost itself in the maze of holding pens and marshalling yards that were ringed by dingy dwellings and roaring hell-houses.

Apache Street had emerged as the main thoroughfare years earlier, was now impressive enough with its imposing courthouse and the two-storeyed prominence of the Cattlemen's Association building, which was flanked on both sides by big saloons and solid-looking stores and shipping houses.

At the furthest point from Apache Street were the marshalling yards, where the neighbouring dwellings of the poorer classes sprawled away untidily, shrouded in the eternal stink and dust of cattle.

This was the grubby sector of the booming cattle trade. The imposing, towering face of the Cattlemen's new building stood on the other side of town. Containing conference rooms, café bar and club, it was the ultimate in comfort and style west of the Mississippi and was Bonito's pride. The bar occupied the entire first floor, for the patrons of the building were hardy drinkers, and the lights mostly burned there until long past midnight every night.

It was these lights which first told Quint Dannecker he was nearing his destination. He reined his black horse to a stop on the crest of the rise which had brought the town into sight, fashioned a cigarette.

The brief flare of the vesta revealed a bronzed, recklessly handsome face with a quirk to the broad mouth. He sat in silence for a full minute with the red tip of the cigarette gleaming in the moon shadow of his hat.

Behind him now lay the high country where the crags and mighty timbers had continuously obstructed his view of the trail ahead. But here, standing like giant black sentinels were pines, gnarled and ancient, and great blue fragrant cedars. There was the sweet scent of the valley, of grass and bluebells. From directly behind upon the wind came the fragrant odour of old trees and the yellow pines which ran all the way down to Sam's Landing.

He flicked the butt away and grunted as the black moved on.

He reached the Bonito River about a mile above the ridge, where the main trail from Oxbend bridged its width. He ignored the open trail and instead stuck to the river. This was the action of a naturally cautious man . . . for one wary of open spaces where a rider might make an excellent target, particularly on a bright, moonlit night such as this.

He travelled on alongside the river with its

trembling rapid sheen under the moon, and the trees soaring against a misty sky, light-streaked where the breeze ruffled the leaves. The wind was cooler here, with a hint of winter upon its breath.

He paused briefly upon emerging from the last of the woods, hard by the mill which was the first building on the outskirts of Bonito. Following a slow look about, he drew the Colt from its holster, spun the chamber to check the loads, then replaced it and kneed the horse ahead.

He began to hum a tune, softly at first then with greater volume. Finally he began to sing, as he often did on the long trails, causing the animal to toggle its ears.

The stage driver from Sam's Landing had reported upon arrival at Bonito at dusk that he had sighted a stranger who fitted Quint Dannecker's description on a high ridge just out of the Landing when he'd been heading out. This news had set the town buzzing and now there were volunteer lookouts posted at vantage points around the town perimeter, each lookout keen to be the first to sight him.

Uncomfortably posted against the wall of a henhouse on O'Dooley's farm, Whiskey Bob Evans was the first to hear somebody singing, then glimpsed the impressive shape of the tall rider crossing the stubbled field towards the mill.

'It's him, by hell!' he muttered, squinting hard. 'Hey, that you, Quint Dannecker? Bob Evans here!'

The singing ceased. A six-gun boomed at the sky, followed by a low laugh.

Whiskey Bob paled, spun on his heels and legged it for Apache Street on stubby legs. 'By all the saints it must be him!' he panted.

He reached the street, sweating and dry-mouthed. He tried to yell out to the staring bunch in the street who were still trying to figure where that shot had come from, and who'd touched it off. He was forced to swallow several times before he could make himself heard.

'He's here, b'God! Quint Dannecker's ridin' up by Dooley's, large as life!'

Forewarned, the official welcoming committee had time to emerge from various saloons and take up their positions before the courthouse. A crowd had already assembled, a large number of men but also many women by the time Quint Dannecker rode into view around the corner of Starbuck's Feed and Grain. Sounded like he was still humming a tune.

Uncertain giggling erupted among some of the drinkers, this developing into laughter. For some reason nobody had expected the arrival to go quite like this.

'By the eternal!' boomed old Tad Macduff. 'He cain't be the same hellraiser he used to be. Never heard him sing a note before . . . he was always too busy raisin' the dust, as I recollect.'

But soon the voice was being drowned out after one man began to cheer and a dozen voices chimed in, and then folks were pressing forward, hoping to be amongst the first to shake the newcomer by the hand.

The old-timers saw at a glance that the man had aged but little since he'd quit. He still looked, as one now aged matron of Bonito had stated publicly and famously a decade earlier, 'The best-lookin' hellion this side of the Mississippi!'

Everybody watched intrigued as he was reunited with brother and father, springing down from the saddle to seize the old man's hand and slap him across the shoulders. Then with one arm around Rick's shoulders he listened with a broad grin to Chad Stanley's carefully prepared speech of welcome.

Were they going to extremes to make the wanderer feel at home, some pondered? They sure as hell were, and it seemed nobody would have been satisfied had it been any other way.

For there was no doubt that most of the usually sober citizens felt that the pinning of the marshal's star on Lige Dannecker's eldest boy would mark the end of the bloodshed, violence and gunplay which had tainted Bonito's reputation for far too long.

Following the welcoming speeches the ever-swelling party moved on to the restaurant room of the Cattlemen's Association building where there was food, dancing if you wanted and good music in the background.

'A fine chance,' as Chad Stanley announced, 'for Quint to reunite with the friends of his boyhood!'

The party rolled on into the night and was still booming boisterously when a formidable figure came charging through the doors to holler, 'Dannecker, you son of a jackass!' It was Buck Silver, and for a moment a deep hush fell over the crowded room and every eye sought Quint out,

At first he scowled hard at the rancher, causing a few timid ones to step back a little. Quint was frowning menacingly as he flexed his shoulders and advanced towards the rancher, and chairs went over as more moved back to give them space. A yard from Silver now, Dannecker halted abruptly, his scowl by this truly ferocious. The crushing silence seemed to last for an eternity before Quint's face split into a huge grin and he clapped the big rancher boisterously on the shoulder.

'Silver, b'God! Uglier than ever, which I never reckoned possible!'

Silver's astonishment gave way to relieved laughter and the two shook hands and pounded one another on the back to the accompaniment of a thunder of relieved applause from very side.

This was a strange sight to see – but who could doubt the testimony of his own eyes?

The welcome home shindig that followed lasted until three in the morning. It was possible that by one o'clock, many had forgotten what they'd been so nervous about, but everyone agreed it was a great occasion. At midnight a normally sober Tad Macduff had to be restrained from climbing on to the roof to flaunt his tap-dancing style – this from a man who could go one whole week without smiling without even trying hard.

At twelve-thirty by the town clock, Emmaline Grover, respectable wife of stiff-necked attorney John Grover gave credence to recurring rumours that he'd orginally met her dancing the can-can near-naked in a house of questionable repute in a bar room in Wichita – when she turned on a wild dancing exhibition that had the boys bawling for more.

Until a red-faced Grover hauled her off the floor and out into the buggy.

Around three, an intoxicated assay agent declared that his wife was flirting with Quint and attempted to drag her from the room. Quint promptly borrowed a set of manacles from the deputy and used them to clip the agent to a roof support while he sobered up then assured his lady she was free to flirt with anyone she liked.

The welcome home was declared a raging success.

Sheriff Ryle Gammel not only rejected the Bonito Citizens' Committee's request to have Quint Dannecker formally sworn in as first deputy of the town, but actually put to paper that he seriously considered the citizens to be out of their minds even to suggest such a thing.

Fortunately for Dannecker, the sheriff didn't have the authority to impose sanctions or restrictions where such matters of law office appointments were concerned, and he was reminded of this without apology.

The following day the Committee joined with Parson Ryedaker and presented themselves at the courthouse, where Quint was formally sworn in as Special Marshal of Bonito at a salary of four hundred dollars per month. The merchants had gagged a little at the suggested salary but with cowboy trouble on the rise and city violence in the squalid quarters of town an ongoing problem, they realized they had little choice.

The first week reassured even the doubters amongst them beyond all expectations.

During that period the citizens of Bonito were not to be left in two minds concerning the abilities of their new peace officer.

Quint was on the street with Rick from morning until night, often as late as three a.m. The jailhouse filled to overflowing and the bench magistrate reported a record in fines.

The new peace officer broke up brawls at the Welcome, the Daisy Chain, the Ignatz and the Golden Hind, cracking several heads and winging two brawlers in the process.

These wild ones survived, but it served to show he really meant business. One day he rode out ten miles to meet an approaching trail drive and warned boss and crew together against over-exuberance or horseplay once in town with money in their Levis. This warning proved so effective that he was obliged to have Rick collar only wild-eyed ranny who couldn't resist the impulse to shoot some holes in the Bird Cage's roof.

It was his handling of the half-breed Kip Darby from the Running S, however, that set the seal on his authority. There wasn't a citizen in town who didn't believe the half-breed had slain Deputy Hart, and they smarted under his flaunted arrogance. His known skills with a six-gun prevented anybody bracing the wild man up until this time, but Dannecker felt no such restriction.

The half-breed and a handful of rannies off the Running S had just started on their first Friday night drink when Dannecker came in through the swinging doors two steps ahead of his brother.

The lawmen paused, speaking in undertones and Rick nodded towards Darby. Everyone noticed that Quint loosened his six-gun in the holster. Then he thrust his hat back off his forehead and crossed to the bar with the easy relaxed walk which had become familiar with the towners over the past week.

Darby scowled a little at all this, yet went on sipping his drink. Two of his pards moved back a pace but the remaining man, a red-thatched and hard-featured waddy named Leary, stood his ground.

Quint drew up before them. He stared hard at

Darby who feigned an intense interest in the whiskey shot in his hand, while Leary glared at the marshal.

In a quiet, casual tone of voice, Quint said to Leary, 'Get your sorry ass away from here!'

Leary's eyes bugged. The order had been issued so casually he could scarce believe what had been said. 'W-what in hell for?' he finally got out. 'We ain't done nothin'.'

Darby turned to watch and listen as Quint went on in the same flat tone, 'I don't aim to tell you twice.'

Leary took a long, careful look at the face of the badgeman and suddenly stepped back to where the other Running S hands had taken refuge in numbers. Darby curled his upper lip in a sneer yet he still hadn't spoken.

All was silent until Dannecker said, 'They tell me you are real handy with that cutter, greaser!'

That last word brought a flash from almond eyes. Darby was a man with a supple and muscular body who moved with the fluency of a mountain cat. He moved that way now to stand before Quint with right hand hooked close to the holster strapped to his right hip, every inch radiating hostility.

Dannecker smiled right in his face.

'You looking to brace me, small-time? Hell, you ain't even half a plateful for a man when it's not black dark like it was the night you butchered Jack Hart. I never knew him but I hear tell Hart was a mighty fine man, and I hate to hear of a good man getting cut down in his prime – I surely do.'

Without a hint of warning, a wild-eyed Darby went for his gun with a half-shout, half-curse.

Dannecker's blurring right hand whipped out his six-shooter which he whipped viciously across the half-breed's hand. Darby howled in agony as his weapon spun to the floor. He had no defence as Dannecker holstered his weapon and delivered a right hook to the jaw, dropping the hellraiser to the floor.

Before anybody could anticipate what he might do next, the new peace officer lifted his boot then deliberately dropped it upon the waddy's outstretched hand – and everybody heard bone crack.

Darby's scream of agony was chopped off as the deputy kicked a right to the jaw and the hardcase went out to the world.

The saloon fell hushed. Nobody spoke. Nobody seemed to breathe.

Then Dannecker stepped back to face the trio of rannies staring disbelievingly at Darby's motionless form amongst the sawdust. They were silent and looked sick.

Darby's voice was calm. 'Get him out of here, Leary. When he comes to, tell him he's real lucky he's still got one hand to do any heavy lifting he might have in mind. You can also tell him this town is off-limits to him for one month. If he shows in that time I'll kill him.'

Without a word, Darby was lifted and toted towards the batwings. Halfway there, Leary dredged up a little courage. 'We're all off Runnin' S, Dannecker. That's Silver's spread, in case you don't know—'

'Tell someone who cares. Get out!'

The slatted doors flapped into silence as the trio vanished into the night with their burden. Danneker turned to meet the mainly admiring stares.

'Let's hope he learns his lesson,' he said quietly. Then he added, 'That everybody does.'

'They sure enough will now, Quint,' a towner declared. 'That there breed won't never be usin' that hand to bust up folks for quite a spell.'

'That's the idea. If somebody had put that paw of his out of action when he first needed it, Jack Hart would still be alive today. Well, we still have a town to patrol. Let's go, Rick . . . hey, where's Rick?'

'He left, Quint.'

'Left?'

'Yeah, right after you stomped that there hand. Looked kinda pale and pukey like, so he did.'

'Do tell?' Quint looked a little puzzled as he headed for the batwings. 'I guess he is still only a kid at that.'

CHAPTER 5

BROTHER MARSHAL

Rick went along the porch, crossed the sandy width of the yard and then entered the welcome coolness of the stables.

The big black horse was still where Quint had left it.

Rick sighed with relief.

This had become a ritual for him now, had been every morning for the two weeks of Quint's return.

Even though his brother was marshal now, and despite the fact that even though he appeared to be totally satisfied with his new occupation, Rick still half-expected to get up one morning and discover the big black horse missing and the room at the far end of the porch, which had always been kept ready for Quint, still and empty.

He went to the doorway and stood with hands thrust into the hip pockets of his Levis.

Early morning sunlight sparkled on willow tendrils over by the tack room and fat hens were exploring the dusty hollows around its walls.

Cocking his head, he could hear Lige in the kitchen and scented the heady aroma of prime bacon frying drifting pleasantly upon the still air.

It was a familiar scene and a typical morning – and yet different as most things seemed around here since Quint came back. It seemed that Quint's sheer energy and dynamic way of going about things and getting them done had altered everything. Nothing was the same again after Quint Dannecker touched it and that included himself and Lige.

He glanced up at the sound of the kitchen door opening on to the gallery. His father's voice sounded from the doorway.

'Breakfast ready!'

'Be there in a minute!'

He returned to the stables and fed the horses. They tallied three now including Quint's black along with the old grey horse which had been a family pet for more than fifteen years and which had not been ridden in the past five, plus his own gelding.

Housed in the stall next to Quint's mount, the gelding appeared even less impressive than usual. It was ten years old with a coat which no amount of currying could persuade to shine. Still, it was a deep-chested and long-winded animal which could always get you where you wanted to go and bring you back, if ever a horse could.

He gave the animals some barley chaff and as a special treat, hand-fed each a dipper of corn. Quint's black accepted the offering with its customary air of aloofness. Rick grinned. He'd never known a horse to suit its owner as well as that black suited Quint. The horse stared down at him arrogantly and Rick could see his reflection and that of the yard mirrored in the moist jewel of the animal's eye.

'Rick!' called Lige from the house.

'Coming!'

He went swiftly across the yard and mounted the porch steps. Quint's door was still closed. He entered the kitchen and rinsed his hands at the basin beneath the window.

Today, all seemed calm and tranquil in the wake

of the violence.

'Eggs?' queried Lige, seated in his chair by the stove ladling fat over a dozen eggs in a skillet.

'Just one.'

He sat and noticed there were but two plates of bacon on the table. 'Quint not eating?' he asked.

'It's his day off, remember?'

'Oh, yeah, I forgot.'

The old man took his plate and lifted a yellow egg on to it with a skillet, moving with that unhurried economy of action he'd always had. The two ate in silence for a spell with the gently burbling coffee and the occasional crackle of a wood chip in the firebox the only sounds.

Rick rose to get the coffee. 'Quint must've been home late last night. He was still out when I came in at one. You see him?'

'Yeah, I waited up. He showed up around two.' Lige took the proffered cup and ladled sugar into the beverage. When Rick was seated again, he went on, 'He got into a wrangle with Buck Silver.'

Rick arched his brows. 'I knew Silver was in town. What was it about?'

'The half-breed.'

'Oh.' Rick set down his cup.

'Yeah. Apparently Buck was away in Oxbend when it happened, but from what I can make out he was none too happy when he found out.'

Rick glanced up. 'Well, that's not surprising.'

His father studied him closely. 'That stuck in your craw a bit, didn't it. Quint roughin' up Darby that way.'

'I never said it did.'

'No, and that's why I'm suspicious.' After a time when Rick had not responded, the old man went on. 'Darby killed Jack Hart, you know, no doubt in the world about that. Don't you figure he had it comin'?'

'Sure, I reckon so.'

'You only reckon?'

'Well, he had something coming right enough, but maybe not what he got.'

He paused to shake his head as if unsure how to put his thoughts into words.

'We're law, Quint and me. Law in Bonito. Somehow I don't reckon it's fitting to handle a man that way. If Darby broke the law, then he should be charged and tried. The laws of the United States took a whole lot of men a long time to work out and agree on. But if every man deals out his own breed of law things will always be in the mess they are now. Leastways that's how I feel. You reckon I'm talking loco?'

'No,' Lige said slowly. 'Matter of fact I reckon

you're talkin' the best sense I've heard in a long time.'

Rick grinned in appreciation of the rare compliment. Then he was sober again.

'But maybe a place like Bonito – or whatever it's become over time – needs Quint's brand of tough marshalling. It sure enough gets results.'

Lige Dannecker took a sip of coffee and sighed gustily.

'Not the way I see it. As you likely know, I was against them sending for Quint from the start . . . much as I wanted to.'

'You don't figure he was right for the job?'

'Not that. He can handle any man, situation or whatever better than most anybody I know.'

'Then why didn't you—'

'My stubborn ways, I guess. You see, I always tried to work the law in with the citizens so that everybody had a say. Quint never worked that way. It's always "His way or the highway" as the saying goes.' The weathered face broke into a grin. 'Maybe you and me are just a bit behind the times, son.'

Rick nodded and rose. 'Could be. . . .' He moved to the doorway and looked out. 'Did he get to tangle with Buck Silver?'

'Nope. He said he just told Silver that men like

Darby couldn't do as they pleased while ever he wore a badge, and after some arguing Buck seemed to agree with him. They went off together to sink a few beers at the High Pocket to show there were no hard feelings, I guess. That's what made him late getting home.'

'Uh-huh. Well, I'd best get down to the office. I locked up two boys from the Lazy Y tonight. They'll be anxious to get out to the spread so they don't get docked a day's pay. Reckon I'll be home around six for supper.'

'See you later then, Rick.'

'Sure – later.'

The hens scattered from his path as Rick made his way across the yard. He found the dusty street all but empty save for Tom Morgan busily loading a mule wagon with hides in an alley, before he swung into Apache Street.

He walked along the plankwalk on the shady eastern side. The town was slowly stirring into life, with several stores and liveries already opened and men from the Town House Boarding Rooms lounging out front with their cigarettes, waiting to be summoned to the breakfast table.

He traded greetings with those he met until he was halted by Varn Tidrick out front of his store. The man was full of news of Quint's clash with

Buck Silver and was plainly hopeful Rick would supply some additional details.

But he didn't. He cut the storekeeper short and headed on his way.

Somehow he just wasn't in the mood to want to discuss Silver today . . . or any other day for that matter. Privately he saw Buck Silver as a rough-rider whom he might have to come down on hard one day, and he didn't like the notion of that man and Quint being friends.

The routine at the office quickly claimed his full attention.

After releasing the two men from the Lazy Y from the cells he yarned briefly with a cowhand who was in jail for the week for failing to ante up with the dollars to cover a window he'd busted when drunk. He then set turnkey Mike Tollis to cleaning out the cell block before going off to the Green Dollar for coffee.

Returning to the office a half-hour later he found Judy Stanley waiting for him.

After trading some small talk, most of which seemed to be about Quint's impact upon the town, with Judy doing most of the talking, she suddenly paused, then said:

'Quint asked if I'd care to go for a drive in the country with him today.'

He stared at her for a moment, off-balance. Then he cleared his throat. 'Are you planning to go?'

'I didn't say yes or no. I told him I'd ask you first.'

'I didn't know you'd got to know Quint so well.'

She smiled disarmingly. 'Oh, naturally I've bumped into him from time to time.'

'So I've heard. You know, it seems I haven't seen you very much myself these past few days.'

'No, you have not,' she pouted. 'You're always stuck in that stupid office. That's why I considered Quint's invitation. I'd just love to get out of the town for a few hours.'

He shrugged. 'Heck, you don't have to ask my permission, Judy. I've got no rein on you.'

'I know that, Rick, but I want you say it's all right if I go . . . for some reason. . . .'

He experienced a strange constriction in his chest at that moment, realized he actually hated the notion of her going any place with Quint. But reminding himself he had no right to feel that way, he smiled and said easily, 'Sure, it's fine if you go. It'll do you both a power of good. Quint's been working plenty long and hard recently.'

She came round the desk and kissed him lightly on the cheek. 'You're a pretty swell fellow, Rick

Dannecker.' She went quickly to the door. 'I'll stop by and see you when I get back.'

It seemed very still and silent in the office after she was gone. He stared down at a pile of reports waiting his attention, papers that should get away on the afternoon stage to Oxbend.

He sat down and got to work, but the number of errors he made in his pen work showed he wasn't concentrating.

After half an hour he gave it best and took to pacing to and fro for a spell before heading outdoors to try and relax on the bench, but without much success. He was there for some time before a porch loafer called across to him; 'Why, lookit, Deputy. Here comes old Quint – in a buggy already!'

He glanced up sharply. The couple in the two-horse, yellow-wheeled buggy were identifiable even at a distance as Quint and Judy Stanley. They made a handsome pair. That was his first impression, the second was that he felt they were seated a little closer together than they might need to be. He swore and tried to appear relaxed as the rig wheeled abreast, still travelling at a brisk clip.

Judy waved gaily, and Quint called, 'Be out at the crossing if you need me, Rick.'

'Sure – have a good time,' Rick replied.

The buggy receded swiftly, followed by the eyes of the street. They made a vividly impressive couple – the petite, fresh-faced young woman and the tall and bare-headed marshal whose white smile flashed at something she said.

As they disappeared Rick realized he was under sharp scrutiny from old Elmer. 'What?' he asked gruffly.

'Weren't that your gal with Quint?'

'Maybe.'

'And you'd let her go buggy-ridin' with him?'

'Why not? Anyway, what business is it of yours?'

Elmer raised both hands. 'Now don't go gettin' ornery with me, boy . . . I was just remarkin'.'

'You talk too much, old man,' Rick snapped, and headed for the doorway.

Before he could get inside he heard the bum muttering, 'Sure wouldn't let any gal of mine go runnin' off . . . not with a feller like old Quint I sure wouldn't. . . .'

He heard no more as he slammed the door shut. Hard.

Later, it seemed that nobody on the Running S Ranch really knew how the fight got started.

What everybody on the county's biggest spread

did know, however, was that the Clanton twins had seemed to show a knack for riling the boss rancher right from the get-go. Amongst the crew were one or two who felt obliged to caution the husky new hands from the south against their disrespectfulness and felt obliged to point out that Buck Silver possessed both a stormy temper and maybe the most punishing pair of fists in the whole county.

The Clantons didn't listen, so what happened at the hay barn on the spread late that afternoon seemed to have something inevitable about it when viewed in retrospect. The twins were pitching hay under a hot sun when the rancher happened by and suggested – or more likely ordered – that they quit dreaming and got working!

It was like touching tinder to a torch. In nothing flat the tetchy twins were shouldering each other aside in their eagerness to get at the slave-driver rancher.

Jimmy won the race and paid for it in no uncertain manner. It appeared to the onlookers that Silver was smiling as the hot-head came in on him with a rush, but there was nothing even vaguely funny about the perfectly timed right hook the rancher delivered dead on target to the point of the jaw. This saw Clanton's lower limbs continue moving forwards while his upper body was going backwards and downwards like he'd been smacked with a shovel.

Jack Clanton saw his brother drop like a typhoid case from the corner of his eye. But he didn't take offence. Jimmy was a fool to go in with his head cocked high that way – he should have attacked the way he was doing right now – head tucked low, shoulders high for protection, right fist cocked and ready to explode like a bomb on the rancher's jaw.

Waiting until the very last moment, Silver delivered a one-two combination with both fists to the jaw then swayed aside with the supple grace of a dancer to allow unconscious twin number two to hit the ground hard, eyes rolling in their sockets.

'OK,' the rancher said easily to the circle of wide-eyed faces around him. 'Nobody said anything about it being time for a break, did they?'

Everybody got back to work and within minutes the twins, still out to it, were sprawled side by side in a buckboard heading for town while the boss of Running S was whistling while he worked. Tall, arrogant and triumphant, Buck Silver in that moment looked nothing like a man who could be riding for a fall.

*

The buggy ride out to the river was just the first of several such outings for Quint Dannecker and Judy Stanley.

With the first eventful fortnight of Quint's role as marshal of Bonito progressing smoothly and his roughshod style of imposing law and order impressing everybody including even the hell-raisers, he suddenly found himself with leisure time on his hands.

He played pool at the parlour with old and shiftless companions from the old days. He went hunting for bear in the hills around the Running S with Buck Silver, and spent many a leisurely hour at the High Pocket.

The fortnightly meetings of the town's Citizens' Committee became a self-applauding society for those who'd had the foresight to send for the town-tamer. They believed he was worth every cent of the high pay he demanded and received.

Much of the credit for this situation rested on the well-tailored shoulders of Committee chairman Chad Stanley, and if Stanley felt uneasy about his daughter seeing a lot of their new town-tamer, he gave no sign.

Rick and Judy called off their casual

relationship in that time. Both studiously avoided mention of Quint's name, yet he stood between them now as noticeably as if he were present in the flesh.

In the vague, dreamy way of the young, Rick had imagined that at some bright time in the future he and Judy would marry and settled down in Bonito – he already had the house in mind.

Now that dream had exploded.

He was hurt, sure, but hardly angry. He could see how any woman might prefer a high-powered personality and local idol like Quint to himself. He himself was, after all, just a lowly second deputy who was regarded as simply too young and inexperienced by the wise men of the Committee to assume the office he really felt he deserved.

Oddly enough, the rift between Rick and Judy made no change to the realationship between the brothers. If Quint was aware there had been a rift, or that he was the cause of it, he gave no sign. He was as close to Rick as ever and that fact alone seemed enough to satisfy both men . . . and to hell with whatever the gossips might be saying.

Lige Dannecker watched the unfolding personal and political events of his town with a more experienced and keener eye than anybody. Maybe he alone knew how much his younger son had been hurt over the collapse of his relationship with Judy Stanley.

He was also aware of a persistent sense of unease about the new way law was being administered in what he still regarded as 'his' town. Like a master chessman watching a game over which he had no control, but in which he held a high stake, Bonito's crippled ex-lawman was a silent spectator from the sidelines. He might have cheered for his favourite to win had he known who was in the right.

Too bad he was no longer sure.

CHAPTER 6

GUNSMOKE AT THE HIGH POCKET

The spidery hands of the banjo clock on the jailhouse wall showed ten minutes after midnight when the flat crack of a shot echoed across Apache Street. Quint and Rick, their boots propped atop the scarred office desk, exchanged one quick questioning glance before swinging their feet to the floor and heading for the door.

Men boiled around the High Pocket, some rushing out, others forcing their way in. One was already halfway across the street when the lawmen emerged from the office.

'Quint . . . Rick!' he gasped. 'There's been a shooting!'

They joined the man, a labourer named Scott, who delivered a rough account of the incident while they were all three making for the saloon.

'They was playin' cards . . . had been for most of the night, Marshal. Nobody seems to have seen perzackly what happened, but seems Silver just—'

'Silver?' they echoed together.

'Yeah,' affirmed the man, eyes wide at the recollection. 'Silver shot the gambler, Roley Thane.'

'Dead?'

'Never seen one deader.'

The man fell behind as the two shouldered through the mob gathering outside and went through the batwings. Like the scene outside, the interior of the High Pocket was one of great confusion. Owner Elmer Stang, his normally high colour inflamed further by agitation, rushed across to them directly.

'Is it true, Elmer?' Rick demanded. 'Did Buck Silver kill Roley Thane?'

Stang nodded jerkily. 'They was playing cards most of the night . . . you seen them earlier yourself, Quint—'

'Yeah, I sure did. Where's Buck?'

'Still at the table,' Stang supplied, jerking a fat thumb at the far end of the bar room. 'I had the boys tote Thane out in back . . . there weren't no need to send for a medic.'

The chandeliered saloon had quietened considerably since the appearance of the lawmen. Now, as they made their way towards Buck Silver's table with Quint leading and Rick a pace behind, the onlookers grew quieter still, sensing the next development in the high drama.

There was scarcely a man present unaware of the friendship existing between Quint and Buck Silver, nor any of them unfamiliar with young Rick Dannecker's opinion of the high-riding boss man of the Running S.

Silver sat straight with his back against the wall, a little paler than usual but showing no signs of remorse. He wore his customary flamboyant frilled shirt and deerskin jacket. His was a face of arrogant strength, long-boned and strong and dominated by a pair of dark, proud eyes. He glanced up at the lawmen challengingly.

Quint halted before the table and extended his right hand. 'Give me that gun, Buck.'

Silver's lips compressed. 'Why?'

'Just give it to me.'

The two traded stares for maybe a half-minute,

and Silver was the one who at last backed down. Scowling, he took out his Colt and handed it butt first to Dannecker. Quint sniffed the muzzle then dropped the piece upon the table with a thud.

'What happened?'

A babble of voices erupted and he raised both hands. 'Quiet!' he said, and when quiet was restored, he nodded. 'I asked Buck what took place. I'll hear the rest of your stories later.' He focused upon the rancher. 'Well?'

Silver leaned back in his chair. 'I was playing cards with that feller from Louisiana – Roley Thane. I won a heap earlier in the night but over the last two hours he took me for plenty.'

'How much?'

'Fifteen hundred.'

A murmur went up. Again Quint motioned for silence. 'Go on.'

'He was cheatin'.'

'How do you know?' demanded Rick.

'Ahhh, the boy lawman.'

'Stow that, Bart!' Quint rapped. 'How did you know?'

Silver snapped, 'Just a hunch.'

'Anybody else see him cheating?'

'There was nobody watching.'

A red-faced wrangler called from the crowd. 'I

seen 'em once or twice, Marshal. Silver looked like he was gettin' mighty riled to me. I—'

'I'm not interested in how things looked to you, mister. I want to know if anybody saw that man cheating. Well?' A circle of silent, shaking heads was his response. He looked at Silver who was glaring hard at the red-faced man. 'What happened then, Buck?'

'He made a move for his gun and I plugged him.'

'He wasn't toting a gun!' several voices cried together.

Quint frowned. 'That so, Buck?'

'I thought he was. He made a sudden move for his shoulder, like, under his coat. I've seen those white-fingered cardsharps at work before, and I wasn't fixing to take any risk of him blasting me with a sneak.'

The silence descended and held for the best part of a minute. Then, with Quint stroking his jaw and frowning, and Rick, hard-eyed and accusing, both stared at the broad-shouldered rancher who responded to their attention with a gesture of defiance. Finally Rick spoke up.

'And did anyone see that, Silver?'

'How in hell would I know? I was busy protectin' my hide—'

'Busy committing murder, you mean!'

'Now, Rick—' Quint began, but the young man cut him short.

'You're not aimin' to call it anything else, are you?'

Silver shouted angrily, 'Don't pay no heed to any snot-nosed kid, Quint. Everybody in the county knows he's threatened to jail me one day. He hates my guts.'

'That's because you'd be a menace to any town on the map, Silver,' Rick retorted.

'Now hold on hard there,' Quint admonished. 'The man is right, Rick. Everybody knows as how there's no love lost between yourself and Buck here.'

'You think I'd can a man just on account I didn't like him?'

'Never said that. It's just that I figure you mightn't be . . . well, impartial. So now – any of you men here see the gambling man make a move for his gun? C'mon now, you were all here when it happened. What did you see?'

No response, as before. Most of the men present looked at Buck Silver, some with dislike, many with almost fear, yet all with respect. For each and every man was calculating the possible after-effects were he to speak out publicly against the quick-tempered king of the Running S, and this showed all too clearly in their reticence.

In the silence that followed Quint turned to his brother.

'Nobody saw it. Nobody saw anything.'

Before Rick could respond a deep voice sounded from within the crowd.

'Pardon me, Marshal Dannecker, but I saw it all.'

All eyes cut to the medium-sized, bearded man as he stepped into full view. Quint eyed him speculatively.

'And who might you be, mister?'

'Name's Carlo Kelloe, Marshal. Folks know me hereabouts.'

'I asked if anyone had seen anything and you didn't speak up, Kelloe. Why not?'

'You asked if anyone had seen this feller make a move for his shoulder, Marshal. I never seen that.'

'You shut your lying mouth, Kelloe!' Silver snarled. 'You never saw anything!'

'Afraid I did.' The man looked directly at Quinn. 'I saw them two arguing, there were heated words and then Silver slapped leather. The other man went down when the shot went off – went down without making one hostile move, as I seen it.'

The mob muttered as the eyes of the Dannecker brothers met. Rick spoke directly, 'So, what more do you want than that?'

'This feller's got a grudge against me,' Silver accused. 'Swore he'd even scores with me first chance he got.'

'Seems like every man and his dog has got it in for you, Silver,' Rick snapped.

The big man lunged and swung a blow. Rick ducked and countered with a chopping right to the face that drew crimson. Then Quint was quickly between them and forcing both backwards with impressive strength.

'Enough!' he said loudly, 'or you'll both answer to me.' He paused as they glared and gave ground, then nodded at Silver. 'You claim this *hombre* has a grudge against you, Buck?'

'You can bet on it. We argued some time back, he threw a punch and I put him down.'

'This so, Kelloe?'

'Yeah. But I wouldn't lie. I saw what I saw.'

'What more do you want, Quint?' Rick demanded. 'You've got a body in back and a witness that saw the killing.'

'Yeah, Rick. But just remember, that could be a witness that might be lying his head off to even some old score.'

'Well, that's for a judge and jury to decide.'

'Not this time around.'

Rick couldn't conceal his astonishment.

'I don't know what you're driving at, Quint. But I'm arresting Silver on suspicion of murder.'

An approving murmur sounded around the echoing room but Quint's strong voice rose above it. 'I'm the marshal around here, Rick.'

'And I'm deputy.'

'Sure, and a right smart one. Which is why I don't want to see you make a hot-headed mistake that might reflect against you later. The way I see this thing, Buck figured the gambler was making a threatening move and he shot him down in self-defence. I'd sooner take Buck's words than Kelloe's. But, Buck, I'm not letting you off free and clear, no siree. You ought to get to ease up a little when you're in town, so to make sure you remember that, I'm making Bonito out of bounds to you for a month. If you show up in town in that time I'll toss you into jail.'

'Won't be any need for you to do that, Quint. I've had me a bellyful of this place for a while.'

Rick stepped forward to stand directly before his brother.

'You can't do this thing, Quint. You can't just make up your own laws as you go along. I'm not saying Silver's guilty or not. But there's no doubt in the world that there is enough of a case to warrant a trial. That means it's your duty to lock him up until he faces the court.'

'I don't see it that way,' Quint responded, steel in his voice now. 'Just on account Buck isn't real popular with a lot of folks here and is worth a lot of money to boot, doesn't mean the law should be twisted against him. Some folks just like to see a big man brought low, whether he be right or wrong. But while I wear this badge I don't aim to see that sort of thing happen on my watch. I posted Buck for a month and that's how it stands.'

The tension in the room was electric. It seemed a long time before Rick spoke.

'Is that your final word?'

Quint scratched the back of his neck. 'Yep, I reckon so.'

Rick quit the High Pocket.

He didn't see either the sympathetic or the approving looks on either side, nor realize that the prevailing mood seemed to favour him. His jaw was set, his eyes only on the doors. He walked slowly and deliberately on his way out, as though he needed to hold himself together for fear he might come apart like something fashioned from wet straw.

*

The gelding whickered to him softly in the half-dark as Rick entered the stables. He murmured to the mount and it quietened. The ancient grey stared at him over its stall door. He patted the animal's silky nose and went to the saddle-rack.

Saddling up in the dark was no novelty, and he was ready for the trail in jig-time, the Winchester scabbard strapped firmly in place. He was about to lead the horse out when he heard the familiar sound of wheels upon the hard-pressed sand of the yard. He motioned the animal to quietness, then eased it back into the stall normally occupied by Quint's handsome black.

'Rick?'

He held his breath. Through the slats of the stall he glimpsed his father at the door with moonlight silvering his hair. He called out again but Rick remained silent. Then, 'I know you're in there, Rick – so don't act the fool!'

He still made no response.

'I know what you're up to, so do I come in and get you or do you quit playing games, mister?'

With a soft curse Rick led the gelding out of the stall and walked out into the yard. Lige sat hunched with his big hands grasping the padded armrests of the wheelchair, glowering up at him. Then the man's gaze focused on his tied-down six-gun, his cowhide jacket and the Winchester lashed to the saddle rig.

'So . . . you're headin' after him then?'

'Yeah.'

'You've been waitin' every chance since Quint posted him, haven't you? You've waited a whole week until Quint got called out of town, on account you knew he'd stop you going out there.'

'So, what are you doing here? You figure to try and stop me going?'

'Do you reckon I could do that?'

'Not tonight, you couldn't.'

Lige raised a hand in a futile gesture, let it drop.

'Rick, Buck Silver's got the whole Running S out there to back him up in any showdown.'

'In other words you're hinting I should let a murderer run free?'

'I'd rather that than see you shot to ribbons.'

'He's got to be brought in, Dad. He killed a man in cold blood. There are men ready to testify against him – good reliable witnesses – and I believe their testimony could see him put behind bars and unable to burn their barns down – or worse. Don't you see I've got to do it.'

Lige sighed. 'Maybe you have at that, boy.' He

was silent as he filled his pipe and lit it. 'This ain't going to set too well with Quint, y'know?'

'Guess not.'

'You'd be overriding his authority.'

'It was him who posted Silver when he should have jailed him, not me.'

'Just his way of doing things, I guess.'

'There's only one right way of doing things, and that's by the book.'

The gelding toggled its ears and stamped a hoof, eager to be off. It was a bracing night and the animal had had little exercise during Rick's busy weeks in Bonito. Rick stroked the animal's neck and studied his father. He was silent, but that didn't necessarily mean he was through talking yet.

Lige grunted as he looked up to follow the quick passage of a grey cloud across the face of the moon.

'The last thing I ever wanted to see was you and Quint maybe getting to cross swords one day. No sir . . . that was one sight this old rider always knew he could live without.'

'I said I'm going after Buck, not that I mean to tangle with Quint.'

'But you know that could happen – right?'

'Well, like you say, he's not going to like seeing

Silver looking through iron bars.'

'Yet you're still prepared to go ahead?'

'Right.'

Lige sighed then wheeled his chair closer. His features were expressionless but his words were eloquent – and reassuring.

'If it helps any, I believe you are doing right . . . which is always about the best thing any man can do, seems to me.'

'Thanks, Dad . . . and it sure helps a lot. So, that makes two of us who agree on what must be done.'

'Three. Judy was here to see me this afternoon.'

'Judy? How come?'

'Just felt like talking, I guess. Spoke a lot about you, and didn't seem too partial to Quint right at the moment, seemed to me.'

Rick scowled.

'She just doesn't know what she wants. Quint's too good for her if you ask me.'

'You still back Quint no matter what, don't you boy? In spite of Buck Silver.'

'I still count him as the number one man in Bonito, Dad. And I don't mean to turn against him over something like this. It's just that he has to learn he can't play fast and loose with the law like he does. But he and me will be as good friends as ever after Silver's trial – you can count on that.'

He swung the horse and was ready to go as his father moved from his path.

'I knew it'd come to this, and so did Judy, boy. She asked me to warn you to be careful . . . so that makes two of us, son. So get going. But make sure you keep sharp and watch your back.'

Rick nodded and rode from the yard, oddly pleased about Judy, even though he felt he'd completely gotten over her long ago. '*Adios.*'

He headed directly for Apache Street, crossed it and followed Bowie until it finally became one with the west trail.

On then, past the marshalling yards where locomotives rumbled by, gasping and clanking through the eternal dust and stink of cattle. Then abruptly the town was in back of him and he let the gelding have its head as he pointed its roman nose towards the Running S.

CHAPTER 7

THE RUNNING S

Warily keeping to the deep moon-shadows of the oaks which lined the course of the trail near the spread, Rick rode directly to the pole gate which carried the emblem of the Running S on a wooden sign board, creaking softly in the uneasy wind.

No sign of movement – just the dim silhouette of a lone steer far off to the right. He passed on through the gate then cut away from the trail to approach the homestead directly through timbered rangeland.

The Running S was the biggest spread in a hundred miles with the house and ranch buildings a further five miles off the main trail.

Headquarters constituted a small group of buildings with two long bunkhouses, tack-rooms, cook-house, corrals and barns. Then, upon a wooded rise overlooking it all, the great white house built forty years earlier by Major Silver and now the home of that cattle pioneer and his only offspring, Buck.

Rick circled the bunkhouses and tethered the gelding amongst a stand of willows fringing the banks of a small natural stream within rifle shot of the headquarters.

As had been the case on his only prior visit to the great spread years earlier, he was deeply impressed by the manner in which everything here seemed to reflect power, prestige and permanence.

He studied the layout from cover over long minutes. His plan was to hijack Silver without arousing the crew. Admittedly most of the men here were just basic working cowhands and saddle-sloggers, yet there were also dangerous others like Darby and Leary to consider.

He'd heard that the half-breed had turned even meaner since his maiming at Quint's hands, if that was possible.

He maintained his vigil for a full half-hour. By

then it had gone ten-thirty and most of the lights had been snuffed out, telling him the crew were bedding down for the night.

He stiffened when three figures emerged from the main house and headed leisurely for the bunkhouse. As they passed a pole lamp he was able to identify the imposing height and rugged physique of Buck Silver.

When the trio disappeared inside he waited a further several minutes without sighting further activity. He got to his feet, toyed briefly with the notion of taking his rifle with him but finally decided that surprise and a six-gun might prove the best allies this time around.

Minutes later found him peering warily over the sill of a bunkhouse window to watch a couple of played-out cowhands preparing for bed.

He moved on, ignoring the slow but strong thud of his heartbeat.

It took ten minutes of ghosting silently from window to window before striking pay dirt. In this room he glimpsed Darby lolling upon a bunk with his greasy head resting against the wall, a cheroot between his teeth and a dirty bandanna wrapped around his right hand.

A cowboy strummed a banjo while another was humming as he studied his sunburnt features in a cracked wall mirror. Everything here suggested unawareness, normality and drowsiness – with no sign of Silver now.

It figured he had to be up at the main house.

He eased away stealthily to vanish into the sparse timber which reached almost to the walls of the building itself.

Silence reigned here.

The bunkhouses were quiet, yet several big windows still showed light. Snake-wriggling belly-flat across a stretch of clipped lawn to gain the western gallery, he crossed soundlessly to a lighted window and peered in.

The room, an eatery of some kind, stood empty. There was a door to the right of the window, and when tested, was found to be unlocked.

Plainly security was no top priority on a spread this big.

Easing inside, Colt in hand, he found himself in a long hallway which he followed warily, ready to run or shoot, depending on who or what he encountered.

But the passageway remained empty of life and he felt almost relaxed by the time he crossed a foyer to focus upon a door which stood ajar and from which drifted the sounds of papers rustling followed by the clink of glass upon glass.

He didn't hesitate. He stepped through the doorway and cocked his .45 with a loud click, which caused the figure at the desk in the centre of the room to twist and glance up sharply.

'Don't move and don't even breathe, Silver! I'm taking you in for murder!'

The rancher's right hand froze bare inches from a half-opened desk drawer. His powerful face was silent and ferocious as he glared across at him in the lamplight without blinking.

'The boy lawman!' he hissed at length.

'On your feet, Silver!'

'You're out of your mind, mister. One yell from me and—'

'And you'll be a corpse. Now get up and get moving. We're leaving together and if you make a single sound you'll never hear another.'

There was steel in Rick's voice and something lethal in his look that curbed the rancher's natural aggression. Silver rose, hitched at his belt, seeming to half-fill the room with his height and breadth of shoulder.

'All right, tinstar! This is your play – so far. What now?'

Rick motioned at the door and they went out and crossed the foyer together. A door banged deeper inside the house and somewhere a dog barked. But the six-gun muzzle rammed against the cattleman's kidneys guaranteed his silence as he was escorted to the unlighted sector of the house, which finally gave on to the gallery where an armed sentry stood silhouetted against the moon.

'Call him over!' Rick hissed as the figure turned.

For a long moment it seemed Silver would rebel. Yet wisdom prevailed and he did as ordered. The lookout came across the gallery wearing a puzzled expression which vanished when Rick came out from behind his prisoner and felled him with one swift cut of gunbarrel.

As the man went down Silver moved fast. He caught Rick in the head with a flying elbow which he followed up with a vicious right hook which missed by an inch when Rick ducked. He bobbed up instantly to deliver a brutal chop to the forehead with the .45 with all his strength in back of it.

Silver sagged and Rick caught the slumping form over his shoulder. He took the gallery steps down, three at a time, legs straining beneath the weight.

Staggering across the dimly lighted yard, his breath soon tearing in his throat, he could scarce believe he'd made it so far – almost all the way now – without all hell breaking loose.

He was about to claim total success before he brought his mount into sight but at the exact moment a harsh voice sounded from his right flank. 'Freeze, Dannecker. Mr Silver ain't going no place with you!'

Rick whirled to see menacing shapes emerging from cover, familiar faces daubed by the moonlight and led by Darby, grinning like a dog wolf with a Colt .45 in his fist.

'I can kill you before they could get off one shot, scum!' he warned Silver.

'Maybe, Dannecker, yet I doubt it. Maybe I'd die, but how long would these boys let you live? Two seconds top would be my guess.'

Rick waved his gun muzzle but didn't shoot in the face of overwhelming numbers. Silver's mocking smile was triumphant as he straightened and snapped. 'Take his gun!'

Darby plucked the .45 from Rick then back-handed him with brutal force. Rick staggered, shook his head clear and focused blurrily upon the man he'd come to arrest, the bitter taste of failure like acid against his teeth. Sure, he knew the odds had been against him from the outset, yet he'd still thought he could pull it off. Now it seemed his critics on the citizens' committee had been right after all. Seemed he really *was* too young for the job after all.

He was bundled indoors where the liquor immediately began to flow . . . his heart sinking each time he met Silver's mocking eye.

Darby and the hatchet-faced Leary stood before him viewing him with a mixture of contempt mingled with grudging admiration.

'Well done, boys!' Silver congratulated them all, raising his glass. 'I figured maybe I was a goner when he got the jump on me. How come you showed up like you did anyway, star-toter?'

Darby smiled, a thin smirk of triumph. 'That new Texan you hired last week, boss. He reckoned he heard a strange hoss nicker across the corrals on the creek side. He even bet us five bucks this was so when we told him he was hearin' things. So we went to take a look, and sure enough we found this strange horse tethered and straight away started searching for the rider – and found this bastard, just in time. So, what's the boy lawman's game anyway, boss man? You find that out yet?'

Silver's smile was feral. 'He came out here to arrest me and haul me back into Bonito to stand trial.'

Leary let out a long, low whistle. 'Why, the

man's got more sand in his craw than brains. So, what do you plan to do with him, Mr Silver? Mebbe you'd best let me and Darby take care of him, huh?'

'No. He goes back to Bonito.'

'Going back?' Darby echoed. 'After what he done . . . you'd still let him go back?'

Silver set his glass down and shrugged off his fine deerskin jacket, features grim and taut now.

'You're forgetting he's Quint Dannecker's brother, and I don't mean to have that one coming after me with that shooter of his right now – which he surely would if this punk was to croak.' He shrugged. 'No, he's going back . . . but only after he's got something to remember me by. . . .'

Silver now stood in shirt-sleeves, tall and powerful in the moonlight. He smiled grimly.

'All right, boy lawman, you're overdue to learn respect for your betters.'

Rick's expression was blank as the bigger man closed in. There was no alternative but to fight and hope, he realized. He began to circle Silver slowly, the bigger man turning easily and gracefully with a poise and balance indicating an expertise at any kind of combat.

Rick threw several feints and was moving easily before the absorbed gaze of the onlookers when a fist came out of no place and grazed his chin.

It could have been a knock-out blow had he not bobbed low at the last split-second.

He countered instantly with a left rip to the mouth, then followed this up instantly with a vicious short, brutal right to the heart that stopped Silver in his tracks – but only momentarily. The man was not simply big, he was tough as teak.

Even so, blood was showing on Silver's face as they circled one another warily, and the hands were no longer jeering his adversary as they'd done at the outset now.

Struck in the face twice in as many seconds, Silver lost his temper and came charging in, saloon-brawler style, relying on sheer size and strength to carry the day now.

As they almost did.

In the space of mere moments Rick absorbed several lightning blows to the head under a barrage of lefts and rights that had the onlookers cheering for their boss man again.

But behind his raised fists as he backpedalled before the furious attack, Rick remained almost calm. His adversary was powerful and skilful, but not without a weakness. The man plainly *expected* to win – possibly because former adversaries had wisely allowed him to do so. As a result Silver's slam-bang onslaught was not bolstered by a high-quality defence. . . .

It was several brutal minutes before Rick was given his chance when his adversary finally dropped his guard to let fly with what was intended to be the knockout haymaker. But Rick knew it was coming, had been waiting for it.

He bobbed under the thunderbolt right and came up swinging a left hook from the floor. The brutal shock of impact jarred his arm up to his shoulder and he instantly knew he'd hit the sweet spot – had likely hit it as hard and cleanly as anybody could.

Silver swayed before him staring at him without seeing him, then crashed to his face and didn't move.

Rick was streaking for the doorway even before the huge form hit the floor and put in three long strides that almost carried him through to the safety of the darkness beyond the reach of the torchlight.

Almost. . . .

One wild swing was all it took to connect with his shoulder, causing him to lurch. They swarmed all over him as he recovered balance. He dimly remembered hammering a scarred face into pulp with a perfectly executed right elbow smash to the cheekbone ... and then he was going down on one knee beneath a fusillade of blows.

A boot crashed into his ribs with agonizing force ... another to the side of the head. Then there was searing pain as a bootheel drove down upon the back of his left hand, followed by oblivion.

Silver blinked from his chair by the hearth. He realized he'd slipped back into unconsciousness maybe for a second or third time only when he heard the dim words, 'Well, do it, don't just talk about it. Finish the sonova off and be done with it!'

Finally coming fully conscious the big man was on his feet instantly to shoulder the man with the gun away from Rick Dannecker slumped in the chair directly beneath the veranda lamp. The hardcase crashed to the floor and Silver aimed a kick at him that missed, largely because the man was still suffering double vision from the punishment he'd taken. Silver shook his head to clear it, then peered at the motionless figure. 'Judas Priest!' he rasped. 'Is he dead?'

'Who cares?' Darby was sporting a jawful of broken teeth in the wake of the wild brawl.

Silver found himself able to stand fully erect now, wasn't staggering any longer. 'I care, that's who. If-if he's dead then so's whoever finished him off. Douse him with water!'

Puzzled faces stared at one another in the lamplight. Silver was often hard to figure, never more so than right now as he fingered his six-gun and looked around with that mean look in his eyes.

'He's not moving,' Silver said harshly, and let the muzzle yawn at Darby who blanched.

'You got to be foolin', boss. . . .'

'Is he dead . . . yes or no?'

'No . . . not yet he ain't.'

'Is he likely to die?'

'Look—'

'You look, fool! This here is no nobody from no place. Sure, I wanted him taken care of. But no worse than that. Why? One reason. He's Quint Dannecker's brother. You maybe want me to explain that to you?'

Heads shook slowly. Few names carried weight in this place but Quint Dannecker's certainly did.

It seemed a long time before Silver appeared to relax, just a little. 'OK, some of you tote Leary out. Somebody else gets Dannecker's horse along the stream. You, Jamieson, go fetch the medical kit from the kitchen. C'mon, damnit, move!'

Silver worked fast, and within the half-hour a groggy deputy was astride his horse with an escort to return him to town, while Silver had his own thoroughbred saddled and ready for him when he emerged from the house, dressed ready for the trail.

Everybody stared. What was the boss man doing?

It didn't take long to find out. They were accustomed to Silver playing every hand and game hard, rarely giving an inch to anybody, anywhere. But he wasn't wearing that iron look right now, when a hand dared ask the obvious question. Where was the boss man going?

'Oxbend is where,' came the reply.

They didn't figure, and Silver rode off alone leaving it that way. Darby rubbed the back of his neck as he watched the figure recede and then it struck him. Silver was running for cover. The night's violence had engulfed Quint Dannecker's brother, and tough Silver was plainly bent on vanishing for a time until things blew over. And the hardcase thought, 'This Quint feller must be somethin' to throw a scare into the big man. . . .'

Next thing he was astride his pony and kicking off to overtake the tall rider just as he reached the title gate. 'Mebbe you better take me with you, Mr Silver? I mean—'

'Maybe you're right.'

'You look kind a peaked, boss man.'

'Mebbe. But once I make Oxbend I'll relax.'

'Why so?'

'Sheriff Ryle Gammel is why. In his view Quint Dannecker is just a low gunshark who belongs in jail. If Quint should come after me on account of tonight, then I reckon I could goad Gammel into jailing him. You see, Gammel's daughter had a big crush on Quint once and she followed him all the way to San Antone one time, and Quint sent her back home. That fierce old star-toter never forgave him for luring her away in the first place, then humiliating her and the old man by sending her packing. He's got six deputies down in Oxbend and he'd like nothing better than to have Dannecker show up there . . . you compre now?'

'Sure . . . plain as paint, boss man.'

Doc Murdoch was old and crochetty and wheezed a lot while working. But once he had quit wheezing and started in talking there was no stopping him, which was when his patient swore and got up from his chair.

'Enough, damnit, Doc! I swear you talk more

folks into hospital with your jawbone than you save with that muck you call medicine.'

'Ahh, how quickly they turn on the hand that saves their lives!' old Doc lamented, giving his pince nez a hasty polish as his patient moved about the room. The door opened and Judy appeared to stare at Rick before throwing her arms about him.

'Oh, honey, we were so worried. Is he all right, Doc? Will he be able to—?'

'Able to crack more heads and get his own cracked into the bargain, you mean?' Doc muttered. 'No, I'd say he's more than capable of doing—'

His words were drowned out as Lige entered the room, his eyes lighting up when he saw his son standing there flexing his shoulders and smiling at his girl.

'Hi there, Dad.'

Lige patted his back and nodded. 'Did you get a good look at that wagon that rolled over you, son?'

'How am I supposed to be able to take a pulse with all this socializing going on?' Doc complained, so the jailhouse visitors stepped back and permitted him to complete his final checkup before he clipped his black bag shut, stuck his hat atop his bald dome and headed for the door.

'Constitution of a goddamn mule,' he growled to Lige on his way out, 'and the sense of one to go get himself beat up this way, if I'm any judge.'

When the three were alone, Rick related his experiences in a matter of fact way, Judy fussing with his bandaged right arm while he talked.

Lige nodded and said slowly, 'So, it was Darby.'

'That's exactly what Quint said,' Judy frowned.

'Quint? Is he back?'

'Got back an hour ago.'

'Where is he now?'

'I'm not sure, but he was sure angry when he heard what happened to you.'

Lige nodded. 'Never saw him so dark as when he heard Buck Silver was responsible for the attack on you. But he said he'd hear it from you personal before he took action.'

'Action?' Rick said. 'What kind of action?'

'Don't bother yourself about that,' Judy insisted. 'Come on, have some of this broth I brought you.'

He hated broth but had to admit he felt much stronger after he'd finished. He felt he was doing even better some half-hour later when the door swung open and Quint came in, bringing an aura of the outdoors with him as he tugged off his

Stetson and frowned hard on seeing Rick's bruises.

'How do you feel, Rick?'

'Fine . . . considering.'

Quint turned to Judy. 'What did old Murdoch say?'

'He says he will be all right.'

Quint seemed to relax at that, although there were still tight creases at the corners of his mouth. 'Just as damn well,' he muttered. Then, cocking an eyebrow at Rick, he said, 'Silver did this, then?'

Rick fingered his swollen jaw. 'No, I dusted him. The half-breed got me with a poker, I think.' He attempted a smile. 'Handled it right well judging by the way I feel.'

'What the hell did you go out there for? I'm surprised you're still alive, man. I'd drawn Buck's teeth, why didn't you let it go at that?'

'Silver killed a man in cold blood, and has got to stand trial. That's why.'

'Hell and damnation, you're as stubborn as the old man. You looking for a medal or something, sticking your neck out that way?'

Rick was starting to grow dizzy. He could hear the anger in his brother's voice. 'Now don't go getting involved in any of this, Quint,' he said slowly, massaging his brow. 'And don't you be thinking about bringing Silver in or—'

'I promise I won't bring him in.'

'You do?'

'Right. I won't have to on account he'll be dead!'

Rick felt his blood run cold, and for a moment was overcome by dizziness. When he looked up, his brother was gone. 'Stop him!' he gasped.

'Don't excite yourself, Rick,' Judy said, forcing him to be seated. 'You mustn't. Quint can take care of himself.'

He could feel the weakness taking over again now. She just didn't understand. He wanted to tell her that Quint had to be stopped – somehow. For, should Quint kill Silver it would be a crime and he would have to take in his own brother. He thought he'd managed to whisper this to the girl as the room seemed to darken, but all she said in reply was:

'Just sleep, Rick. Sleep and everything will be all right. . . .'

CHAPTER 8

DANNECKER LAW

There were two guards and a secretary to protect County Sheriff Ryle Gammel from unwelcome intrusions, but there was no stopping tall Buck Silver when he was good and riled.

'Ah, Mr Silver,' a bespectacled clerk said uncertainly, getting to his feet as the towering figure entered. 'I'm afraid the sheriff is far too busy to see—'

'The hell he is,' Silver rapped. 'I mean to see him and I mean to see him now!'

The deputies appeared together in the doorway to the inner sanctum. On a previous visit Silver had revealed himself as both a man of stature and personality. But trailed by the evil-featured Darby now, and with a mean glitter in the eye, he presented a picture which caused the pair to back up sharply.

Silver glared challengingly, the light spilling on to his powerful face which still showed marks that were a legacy of Rick Dannecker's fists. He swung back upon the secretary.

'Well, damnit?'

'Surely, Mr Silver, a man of your eminence must understand the administrative necessities a county such as this places upon the—'

Silver's clenched fist slammed the desk top and everything jumped, including the clerk.

'I want to see Sheriff Gammel and by God I will do just that—'

The inner door swung open and Sheriff Ryle Gammel stood there, bulky and belligerent with thick legs akimbo and an unlighted cigar clamped between meaty jaws.

'What in the tarnal is going on out here? Ahhh . . . so it's you, Silver. I might have guessed. So what in tarnation do you want . . . except maybe a twenty-four-hour watchdog to keep you out of mischief?'

'Whatever it is I want, I don't plan to talk about

it in front of the whole town!'

Gammel, all bluff and bluster but with no grit in his gizzard, seemed to deflate. 'Huh? What's the matter?'

'In your office . . . now!'

With a shrug the sheriff went back inside with the two uneasy men off the Running S trailing. It was a large over-furnished room with lithographs of Grant and Sherman on the walls. There were numerous photographs of the vain sheriff caught in a variety of staged poses. The man attempted to fall into one of these postures when he got safely back behind his huge desk, but Silver was unimpressed.

'He hasn't shown up,' he snapped.

'Who hasn't? Come on, don't shilly-shally, man!'

'Quint Dannecker, damnit!'

'Ahhh, yeah . . . Dannecker.' The sheriff appeared to deflate. 'Say, you know what that dude done once? He lured my sweet, innocent little daughter away with him with his lies and sweet talk and—'

'That's history. I'm talking about the here and now.' Silver towered before the desk. 'There's been no sign of him in the five days I've been here ever since we heard he'd quit Bonito!'

'So?'

'So, where is he, damnit? He's got to be here in Oxbend.'

'Here? Impossible. I'd know about it if he was.'

'He's got to be here . . . waiting!'

'Waiting? What for?'

Silver almost ground his teeth in frustration. 'What else? To kill me, you fool!'

'A man of the worst possible type,' Gammel lamented, yet without an ounce of conviction. Then he jumped to his feet and began circling the office, booming out his antipathy for Dannecker and all his 'gunslinger breed'. Yet his words and actions were somehow out of kilter, and every so often he would pause in mid-sentence to stare vacantly at nothing, before slapping his leg and starting up again. Still talking, he flung himself back into his big fat chair, then almost instantly leapt erect again to pose with his hand thrust inside his double breasted shirt, like Napoleon.

'So?' he challenged.

'So where is he, damnit? He's gotta be here in Oxbend.'

'Here? Impossible!'

'I say he's here . . . waiting.'

'Who?'

Silver stared. The lawman seemed to be slipping

in and out of reality. 'Dannecker, damnit! The goddamn marshal from goddamn Bonito who's aiming to kill me.'

'A man of the very worst type,' Gammel repeated solemnly. But it was plain he was drifting again when he began muttering imprecations and punctuating them with sudden shouts and wild gesticulations.

With fingers pressed to his eyes now, Silver allowed him to rant on. How had he got into this crazy situation, he puzzled? Maybe he would have been better off attempting to make his peace with Quint . . . anything would have been better than this. And yet on that first day Gammel had come over as reasonable and helpful. The lawman had listened sensibly to his version of affairs then immediately offered asylum to Silver and Darby both. He'd even ordered his deputies to keep a sharp lookout for the Bonito marshal, just in case he showed. At the time this had seemed an adequate safeguard, but with five dragging days gone by and with the only word on Dannecker being that he had left Bonito alone and was likely headed for Oxbend, it seemed anything but adequate now.

He finally took his hand from his eyes. In an instant Gammel had ceased ranting and looked as calm and collected as any man could be, so unpredictable had his moods become.

'You really have nothing to worry about, Mr Silver. Were Dannecker to as much as show his nose here in Oxbend he'd be in jail. Special Marshal? Him? He's a gunfighter and I'd treat him as such, by the eternal!'

'Are you dead sure you've heard nothing of him?'

'Not a word. Of course, you realize he could be long gone some place else . . . a hundred miles gone. . . .'

'Not this one.' Silver was grimly convincing as he rose from his chair, iron-jawed yet suddenly weary. 'Best be moving. . . .'

'Er, before you go, Mr Silver.' Gammel grunted as he heaved himself erect and came around the desk. 'As you may or may not know we're preparing to send a delegation to the capital shortly to argue for greater amenities and benefits for Oxbend County. Naturally, such benefits would cover your fine spread . . . and, well, delegations cost money and a donation would be more than acceptable.'

'You want a donation . . . from me?' Silver was cynically impressed by the man's nerve. But then he shrugged. 'OK, you've got it. On one condition. That is, you bring Dannecker to book and see to it he doesn't trouble me again. Ever. Do that and you'll get a donation that will make your eyes pop.'

'A deal, sir. I feel I have earned that donation right now, for my instincts tell me your man will show up here and when he does he'll be in my cells before he knows what hit him. I can feel that in my bones.'

'We'll let it go at that then, Sheriff.' He nodded to Darby, and together they walked out into the dying sunshine.

He wasn't sure what he'd hoped to achieve with Gammel, only knew he hadn't got it. The man had failed badly since he saw him last – as had so many of his former supporters.

The streets and alleys had turned dark and gloomy whereas they'd been soaked in bright sunshine upon his arrival, thanks to the fat lawman's long-windedness. He shrugged and glanced each way along the street, then as he went down the steps he was aware he'd rarely been so edgy, couldn't figure why. Could be there was danger in the air, always a possibility for someone who lived close to the edge like he did. This town might be capable of concealing a dozen Danneckers, and that was difficult to ignore. For, maybe better than anybody, he knew what Dannecker was capable of. Never in twenty years had he known Quint to overlook any injury, treachery or a breach of faith. It was an odds-on certainty he wouldn't ever overlook something like this.

'We have a drink, Mr Silver?' suggested Darby.

'Not tonight.'

Darby looked sulky. 'So . . . back to the house again?'

'Yeah, straight back to the house.'

He went down the steps and nodded to the deputy. Then he and the half-breed continued on along the street before turning into a poorly lighted alleyway. Silver had come to know most of the back alleys and byways of Oxbend over recent days, purely as a matter of necessity. The lane they followed now ran for a crooked quarter of a mile, passing the entrance to the big, Mexican-styled stone villa where he was lodged.

Some distance down the alley he paused to glance behind, then they went on.

They didn't speak. The enforced role of fugitive suited neither man, Silver in particular. He was by nature gregarious, glad-handed, noisy in drink and cursed by an explosive temper that had nearly cost him his life on several violent occasions. His temper was also shorter these days, and when he rapped his shins against some unseen object now, he cursed violently.

Immediately running footsteps sounded behind and Darby emerged from the gloom.

'You all right, Mr Silver?'

'Of course. Back off, damnit!'

'Sure, Mr Silver.'

They went on, their footsteps echoing against high adobe walls and down dank side passageways where silent cats ignored their intrusion.

'We're getting the hell out of this stinking town!' Silver suddenly exploded.

'You mean it, boss?' Darby sounded eager.

'Damn right. I wasn't meant to live like a goddamn rat. I must've been a fool to cut and run.'

'That's the spirit, boss. We're safe at the ranch . . . could stand off a goddamn army there if we had to.'

Their steps grew lighter now and Silver strode on purposefully, his mind already buzzing with plans to return to his cattleman's castle. Maybe, he mused, he would send an emissary to Quint, explaining everything that had occurred and arranging an armistice. Or, failing that, use his influence with the merchants of Bonito to have

Quint removed from the post of marshal.

A few silver dollars in the right place should take care of that easily enough.

By the time they reached the gloomy branch lane leading to the rear entrance of their lodging house he was formulating plans to hire a killer to deal with Quint, once and for all. There was always the right man some place if you searched carefully then flashed enough of the folding money around.

The rusted wrought-iron gate with the bob wire crown loomed before the pair in the dusky gloom. Darby stepped ahead to open it. He tugged and banged for a time without result, finally bent low to squint through the latch-hole. He cursed. 'It is locked!'

'What? Can't be. Here, let me take a look.'

Silver applied his power to the gate but it refused to give. He drove his boot in impotently. It seemed suddenly quiet in the alleyway – unnaturally so. There was no sound from behind.

Instinctively Silver slipped his hand inside his deerskin jacket and drew out his handsome silver Colt. Taking his cue, Darby palmed the iron he wore on his left hip. Still no sound from in back of them.

'Hello there!' Silver called.

No response.

The darkness seemed to grow deeper and Silver felt the bite of the night air more keenly than before. With Darby a tense, half-crouching shape at his side, his instincts warned of danger abroad in the fetid air of the alleyway now. A leaf from the giant elm at the rear of the house fluttered down, causing both men to twist sharply as it fell to ground, rustling.

Silence again.

'It's Dannecker!' Darby decided. 'He's got to be here. He set this up!'

Silver leaned against the gates, beginning to sweat a little now. They couldn't climb out of this dead end; the walls and gate were too steep and high. This realization had a sobering effect on the feral Darby but Silver was made of sterner stuff. Even so, the gunman felt a flicker of uncertainty as he stared up at the high walls and the dark stirring trees, and thought, 'Perfect spot for an ambush.' The revolver in his right hand flicked this way and in search of a target, but found none in the gloom.

Then, suddenly came the shout; 'Come on out, Silver! I've holstered my gun!'

Dannecker's voice sounded close and clear.

'Can we talk, Quint?'

'Too late for that. But I'll face you on even terms. Can't do better than that.'

'I didn't cripple the kid!'

'That's the only reason I'm giving you an even break. Show yourself!'

Silver slipped the Colt up under his coat on the blind side. 'I'm holstered too, Quint,' he lied. 'I'm coming out and it'll be the best man who wins!'

'A deal.'

He moved warily to reach the corner where he glimpsed the dim motionless silhouette beyond. Cold sweat trickled down his collar as he eased foward until he could finally see that Dannecker's hands were empty!

Instantly he sucked in a huge breath and whipped out the silver Colt so fast that he felt one split-second's exhilarating sense of triumph. Then he realized that, incredibly, his enemy had come clear and now his gun muzzle was erupting with yellow gunflame. As the alley rocked to an insane roar of sound he was driven backwards to crash into a cowering Darby, then fell to his knees as though in prayer.

He tried to speak as he toppled but the whole world was filled with gunblasts and he never felt the dank earth against his face.

The victor stood motionless wreathed in gunsmoke, listening to Darby sobbing in terror like a girl.

CHAPTER 9

DEFIANCE

Turnkey Mike Tollis appeared in the office doorway. 'He's back, Deputy, sir.'

Rick glanced up from the papers on the desk. Much of the swelling had gone from his face but several dark marks still showed beneath one eye and along his left jaw. 'Where is he?'

Tollis moved in to lean his hip against the desk. 'At your pa's. Got in half an hour back, so Lige tells me. Never said nothin' though – just moseyed off and hit the blankets, so he did.'

'Then it'll have to wait until he wakes up,' Rick mused aloud. 'OK, obliged, Mike. You can head on home now.'

'Er, your pa says he'd like to see you when you get a minute, Deputy.'

'Right.'

Tollis frowned and indicated the yellow telegraph slip upon the desk. 'That there another wire, Deputy Rick? Not more about the shootout up at Oxbend, is it?'

'No. Could be we've heard all about what happened last night by this.' He tapped the sheet. 'No, this one is from the capital. Judge Reeves is on his way down here, should arrive some time tomorrow.'

'Reeves?' The deputy frowned. 'Ain't that the feller the committee's been at for months to come down here and decide if we're to be granted a town patent?'

'The same. I wired him three days back and followed with a letter. I made it pretty strong, and now it looks like it might have done some good if he keeps his promise to do something about Bonito.'

Tollis smiled, something he rarely did. 'Why, that's great news, Deputy, just great.' He broke off with a sudden frown. 'Three days ago, you say? But Quint only cut loose on Silver last night. How—?'

'I reckon I knew it would happen, Mike – that's how come. Guess it couldn't help but happen the way it did. And if I'm still guessing good, Sheriff Gammel will come huffing and blowing into town at any time, after Quint.' He smiled cynically and it hurt his mouth. 'So, looks like everything's running on well-oiled wheels – heading straight to hell.'

'This don't sound like you, boss.'

Rick rose smoothly and made his way across to the window overlooking the main stem. Cute young mothers out pushing prams; old guys soaking up the sun on Delancey's porch; Jim Croker rolling by in his big old wagon, carting coal. This was his town, but only one side of it. If it was all this peaceful he could get rid of the badge and go fishing.

'Nothing sounds the way it should these days, Mike.' He shrugged. 'But it'll get better, just wait and see. But it's been a long night, could be you should get home and grab some sleep.'

'Fix you some coffee before I go?' He waited until Rick shook his head, made for the door. 'OK, Deputy boss man, and make sure you take it easy. Everything will work out just fine – as my old granny might have said if she hadn't gone off ridin' with Custer, heh, heh!'

Rick's smile faded after the other had gone. For deep down he doubted everything would work out in this man's town either now or in the future, the way it was going. He wanted to believe in tomorrow more than anything, but was no dreamer.

He read and reread that wire from the capital. At least this was some achievement, he felt. In his letter he had warned that if things were allowed to continue as they had been, disaster could result.

They obviously took him seriously, didn't seem worried about his age.

The way he saw it was that, freed from interference and often dominance from Oxbend, Bonito could make its own way forward – elect its own law officers without being forced to hire gunmen and call them special marshals – that was a chart map for disaster.

Sure, they might need to hire a gunfighter for sheriff; he couldn't contest the logic in that. But not Quint, and not Quint's breed of gunfighter either. He held Quint above just about anybody, yet try as he might could not nominate a suitable or practical occupation for his brother. The other possessed ability, courage, charm, integrity and popularity – all the qualities most men aspired to but rarely came close to achieving. The huge drawback for him was that he was a born loner, a fierce and dedicated independent who could never conform to the regimentation of a town like Bonito or any place else.

With a windy sigh he stuffed the wire in his shirt pocket, rose and walked in back. It was only his second day out of bed and he moved stiffly and with some pain. Yet his bruises were healing fast and he could use his right hand OK if not with complete freedom as yet.

He splashed water over his face from the crockery wash basin by the cells, blinked at his image in the cracked mirror in the hope he might look a little older and more mature. No such luck. He grinned and was brushing his hair when Mike Tollis burst into the office farther along the passageway.

'Deputy! They're a-comin'!'

'Gammel?' he said sharply.

'Uh-huh. And with a whole bunch of deputies. Maybe half a dozen.'

Calmly Rick set the comb aside and stared at his image in the glass. 'OK. Go tell Lige. Tell him to wake Quint but warn him not to come horning in. I'll handle Gammel my way. You tell him that and make sure he believes it.'

Tollis vanished. Rick turned and went through the archway to the office. Unhurriedly, he took down his shell belt from a wall peg and strapped it on, thonging down the holster on his thigh. Donning his hat, he quit the room.

Apache Street was rapidly filling, with all eyes focused on the trail to Oxbend. Visible beyond the rooftops, a tan column of dust stained the blue sky. Moments later, the sheriff of Oxbend and his deputies swung around the hardware store corner and rode in fast towards the law office.

Rick stood alone on the porch, the afternoon sun uncomfortably hot upon him. The posse from Oxbend also appeared hot – hot and angry.

Sheriff Ryle Gammel led the troop, massive and dignified with his outsized white sombrero, knee-high cavalry boots and an elaborately tooled shell belt strapped around a sagging paunch.

He slewed his mount to a halt before the law office and lifted his gloved hand to bring the riders behind to a stop as well. Mike Tollis had been right. There were six of them, all armed and unsmiling.

Gammel slumped, round-shouldered, glaring from fat-pouched red eyes. He finally spoke; 'You're his brother, ain't you?'

'Whose brother?'

'Don't bandy words with me, you whelp!' Gammel bawled. 'You are the brother of that back-shootin', womanizin' polecat, Quint Dannecker.

So, where is he hidin'?'

Rick felt his anger mount, and the emotion gave him added strength. 'Reckon I don't know, Sheriff. But if I did, I wouldn't be telling you.'

Gammel turned even paler at that. He glared up and down the street, noting the large crowd that had assembled. The heavy head swung back to Rick.

'You, sir, are insubordinate. I put that badge on you there and, by glory, if you don't show more respect befitting an officer I'll rip it off you.'

'No, you won't, Sheriff.'

Calmly, Rick drew the yellow telegraph slip from his breast pocket. 'I have here a message from the capital stating that Judge Reeves is on his way here and should arrive by tomorrow. When he arrives I plan to have him listen to evidence concerning the shooting in Oxbend, which everyone knows was not murder. He's going to listen to our arguments that we be granted a town patent. In the meantime, Sheriff, I'll rely on you not to disturb the peace.'

'The peace—!' Gammel's words seemed to snag in his throat. He motioned to a deputy who dismounted and came to the steps to take the wire. Gammel studied it, then screwed it into a ball and hurled it away from him across the street.

'We've come here for your brother, Deputy, and we won't be leaving without him. He not only shot and killed two citizens who had come to me in terror of him, but he assaulted a deputy of my force.'

'Those citizens you speak of, Sheriff, were both men who have committed murder in this town in recent months. Silver shot and killed an unarmed gambler named Roley Thane, while Darby claimed the life of the late First Deputy of Bonito, Jack Hart. They are your so-called terrified citizens!'

Gammel's eyes rolled crazily. 'Disarm him!' he choked.

Movement stirred in the Oxbend ranks, but Rick was moving faster. Despite an injured hand he drew smoothly and punched a bullet so close to a rider with a revolver in his hand that the man felt the hot airwhip of its passage and dropped his weapon in fright. Rick cocked his Colt again and angled it at the others. But nobody was going for a gun now. He pumped another shot into the sky then deliberately housed the smoking piece, a gesture of both authority and defiance.

'You're already guilty of civic unrest, Gammel. You're not taking Quint, and you wouldn't take him if he was guilty a dozen times over. This is

Bonito and I am the law.'

'Damn right he is!'

All heads swung in the direction of the loud voice. Quint Dannecker, looking rested and refreshed, emerged from the crowd over by the High Pocket. He was in shirt-sleeves, with the sun glinting off the slanted shell belt slung across his hips. 'You make one hell of a racket, Gammel. Damned if you didn't wake me up.'

Deputies and townsmen alike seemed to freeze. But at the centre of the drama, Rick, Gammel and now Quint Dannecker stood together forming a formidable tableau. Rick held the still-smoking six-gun at his hip. He'd not wanted Quint to play any part in this affair, but then decided it was likely just as well he had appeared. The deputies might have been tempted to take this further before, but he would bet money that Quint's presence would prevent any bloodshed now.

Gammel stared bleakly from face to face, his expression twisted and sick-looking. But he made no foolish move and his gun stayed in its holster.

'You'll hang for this, Deputy,' he whispered hoarsely.

'We've talked enough, Gammel. You and your men can remain in town until the judge arrives providing you swear not to disturb the peace.'

Gammel's face appeared sick and pockmarked as he shook his fist at the wall of onlookers. 'You'll all pay for this, you pack of Judas dogs!'

He twisted in his saddle to address his men. 'We're leaving. We'll trail-camp tonight. This stinking Gomorrah is no fit place for an honest man to lay his head.'

The riders were turning away as he pushed his horse closer to the tall figure of the deputy.

'You are no longer a deputy of Oxbend County, Dannecker. When Reeves is through with you I'll swing you and your gun-tippin' brother on the one scaffold.'

With that he raised his right hand and led the Oxbend party out of Apache Street at the run. It wasn't until the drumming of hoofbeats had faded that the crowd began to mill, talking breathlessly, gesticulating. That had been a close thing and everybody knew it.

Rick was surprised to look down and realize the gun was still in his hand even though the danger was long gone. He put the piece away wearily. Across the street, Quint was being surrounded by admirers, applauded for the part he'd played.

But no committee member or substantial citizen added his voice there. They were relieved that nobody had been slain in this confrontation, but the role Quint Dannecker had played in the showdown didn't set well with the man in the streets, and it showed.

It didn't bother Rick, however, even though he would have preferred his brother stay out of it.

He pushed through the mob out front of the jailhouse and walked away down Apache Street. He wasn't ready to talk to Quint yet. But soon he would have to, and what he would say would be hard for them both. But that could wait. Right now it was enough just to know nobody had been killed.

Judge Reeves studied Sheriff Gammel over the tops of his wire-rimmed spectacles. 'You personally viewed the bodies soon after the shooting, Sheriff? In the alleyway itself?'

'Yes, Judge.'

'And the dead men were armed?'

'Yes, sir.'

'And they actually had weapons in their hands that had been recently fired, did they not?'

'Yeah, but—'

'That will do, Sheriff.' Reeves settled back in his courthouse chair. He was old as ancient parchment and twice as dry. His eyes were a pale blue, surrounded by deep wrinkles in the leathery skin of his face. He was thin and bent but there was a sharpness about him that belied his age. He had a wide reputation as the best justice in the capital, which indeed he was.

He addressed the assembly in general. 'While I abhor the bloodshed and loss of life involved here, I can find no evidence to indicate that it was anything else but a gunfight stemming from a thirst for reprisal on the part of the Special Marshal of Bonito, Quint Dannecker, following the brutality visited upon his brother, the Second Deputy.'

'But, Judge—' began Gammel, but was cut short.

'Sit down, Sheriff Gammel, you are out of order!'

Gammel sat and the gathering in the courthouse relaxed. It was plain the judge had analysed the recent events involved here and had made up his mind what had taken place, and why. This was not a trial but rather a hearing. Present were the members of the Bonito Citizens' Committee, the deputies from Oxbend, three clerks and assistants of the judge's party, Quint and Rick Dannecker.

Rick sat at a table by the bench while the chair opposite was occupied by Gammel. The remainder of those present occupied bench seats, with the exception of Quint. With one leg swinging to and fro and his back to the back wall beneath a window, he sat relaxed and totally at ease with just the ghost of a smile on his face.

Reeves studied his notes and made a few terse observations about such matters as 'frontier justice' and 'six-gun law'. But it was soon plain to all that he was not about to find there had been any miscarriage of justuce, regrettable though recent events had been.

Alone at his table, Gammel seemed to shrink into himself as the judge droned on again, his eyes glazing, right hand thrust inside his flashy vest like Napoleon viewing a defeat on the battlefield. Those who knew him well were accustomed to Gammel being incisive, quick-witted and highly dangerous – at most times. At other times, like now, he appeared to slip away into the limitless world of the dullard, ineffectual, yet still latently dangerous.

But if Gammel were dreaming, the judge was suddenly all business again. He set his pen down and leaned back almost engulfed by the thick black robes encompassing his slight frame.

He had an announcement to make and it revolved around a submission in writing made by Deputy Rick Dannecker in which he formally stated that to improve the law and order situation here, he considered it time Bonito cease to be a mere mandate of the larger town of Oxbend but be granted a patent and become an independent town in its own right.

This set off some hectic debate but in the wind-up the judge prevailed, a vote was called for and the patent duly outlined on paper ready for dispatch to the county capital for consideration.

The building rocked to applause and it was the best part of an hour before the beaming judge decided the meeting had run its course and everyone began filing outside after his closing speech: 'By the power invested in me by the United States Government I shall insist that the town of Bonito be declared, and that all parties present shall be signatories thereof, so help me God!'

There was a prevailing feeling of achievement and goodwill as everyone filed out. Rick was last man to leave, somehow not able to share the prevailing exuberance. Sure, he was pleased and relieved the judge had handled things so well, yet looked and acted like a young man with weighty matters on his mind.

As he walked by the judge and his secretary, the latter observed, 'A fine type of young lawman, wouldn't you agree, Judge?'

'That's how I see him, Clancy,' Reeves said thoughtfully. 'But he has a king-size job before him here, and I don't envy him. There could be difficulties.'

'I've a suspicion you're thinking of his brother, sir?'

'And you just could be right on target, John, I regret to say. . . .'

CHAPTER 10

'QUINT - GET OUT OF TOWN!'

As Firsty Deputy Jack Hart had done in the past, Rick Dannecker attended a meeting of the Bonito Citizens' Committee, the last week of the summer.

Back then, Jack had stormed out of the meeting, frustrated and disappointed by the corruption, ineptitude and avarice he'd witnessed there, resolving to pursue his work as lawman the best way he might without being either helped or hindered by a squad of frightened merchants who characteristically turned to water whenever the wild men of Bonito cut loose.

But Rick felt he had one big advantage over his predecessor as he sat on the right of Chad Stanley at the head of the long table, for he believed he'd achieved more in one afternoon than the present members together had done in years.

True, it had been obvious that Judge Reeves had come to town with the intention of granting the town its own patent. But that had only come about as a result of Rick's initiative in wiring him with both the suggestion and plan beforehand.

It was also a fact that, as a peace officer and a successful one – up to a point – he'd developed more initiative and dedication to his tasks than anybody preceding him.

Despite his failure to bring Buck Silver in from the virtual fortress of his powerful spread, his attempt had at least won him wide support. At the same time it added fuel to the dissatisfaction with his brother's style and method of enforcing the laws.

Quint, who for a short, exciting period had been Bonito's golden boy, was now being closely scrutinized and found wanting.

The meeting followed its usual format: the reading of previous minutes, discussion of matters of finance and an application by Mallory Turnstiles to open up a new saloon and gambling hall down by the stockyards. The minutes, the finances, and particularly Turnstiles's application, received scant attention and were dismissed with minimal fuss.

Chad Stanley immediately took the opportunity then to speak of the day's events with emphasis on the role the deputy had played.

This won enthusiastic support and for several minutes members spoke freely with Rick, offering their personal congratulations for work well done.

Then Stanley rapped the table for silence and it was plain to see that what he had to say was serious.

'Gentlemen, this has been a big week for our town, but it's also been a time to take stock. To ask where are we headed, and what is our destiny? And if we don't answer these questions, who will?'

This drew applause accompanied by sideways glances at both Lige and Rick as the speaker continued.

'Changes create changes. What was good six months ago may not be good now, and what was essential for our safety and security then may well be inadequate now.'

Plainly he was leading up to something important, and they were not left long to wonder what it might be. The impatient ones wanted him to stop talking and get to the nugget of it, and to their surprise, that was just what he did.

Moving on from the general, the address grew specific in regard to Buck Silver who, although having been posted by the special marshal, was considered by many to have warranted arrest and a murder charge brought against him.

This statement drew some applause, and so emboldened, the speaker raised the matter of the friendship existing between their marshal and Silver, a relationship believed to have played a significant part in recent gunplay and bloodshed, thus bringing down the wrath of the Oxbend authorities.

Rick glanced across at his father. Lige sat stony-faced, big hands resting upon the polished table before him as Stanley continued.

'It is plain, fellow committeemen, that we have no option but to invite the resignation of Special Marshal Quint Dannecker in the interests of stability and harmony upon our streets.' Here the speaker paused to study each member in turn. 'I will now invite the members to vote on this, and you may signify your agreement by raising the right hand.'

It seemed all eyes were upon Lige. For a long moment he sat motionless, then his hand went up.

Five others immediately followed suit.

'It will be so transcribed that the vote was passed unanimously,' the speaker intoned.

'May I speak, Chad?'

'Certainly, Lige, go ahead,' Dannecker looked sternly at the man.

'Have you figured how to dismiss him yet?' asked Lige.

'Usual way, I guess. I propose merely to inform him that his services are no longer required.'

Lige leaned back in his chair.

'He won't go.'

All showed surprise. Rob Ramsey said, 'How do you know that?'

'I could see this comin' . . . saw it right after he posted Silver. But he insists he acted within the law when he started shootin', claims it would be a reflection on his ability and integrity if he was put off just for doin' his job.'

'Well, we'll just have to be firm with him,' sputtered Prescott.

Lige smiled tiredly at that. 'Yeah, you should try that sometime, Jake – but only if you've got your affairs in order. You see, Quint suspects he's going to get stabbed in the back . . . and I can tell you that gettin' rid of the man could be a damn sight tougher than signin' him on was. You got to understand that with a guy like Quint, pride is everything. You damage that pride, and you wind up with a damaged man on on your hands.'

The members digested this and then open debate broke out. Rick, listening to it all, felt a cold tightness in his belly. For he'd sensed this could come to pass, and why. He knew his fellow citizens. Sure, they had the town's welfare at heart, worked hard to support it. But they were essentially small men and small men hate anyone rising above them. Quint had risen fast and spectacularly, so much so that they now felt much smaller by comparison. Little men with big egos didn't like feeling that way.

Then came support from an unexpected quarter when, after listening intently to the to-ing and fro-ing on whether to sack or not, Rick came erect, demanded silence and got it.

What he had to say was hurting him even before he'd said a word.

'I sure don't agree with all that's been said here, yet I guess I go along with most of it. Quint's got to go. I've felt that ever since he clashed with Darby at the High Pocket that night. But I guess Dad is right about the way Quint feels – he won't shift until he's ready and by that it could be too late.'

They stared at him with worried faces.

'What do you propose then, Rick?' he was asked.

He took a deep breath. 'Post him.'

'*Post Quint?*'

'Sack him and post him out of town . . . it's the only way.'

They argued, wrangled, reasoned, each with a seemingly different opinion to all the others. The only silent man was Rick himself. He'd not made his decision in a hurry. All along, he'd known Quint could only be effective and practical for just so long. For he was not a lawman but a gunfighter and a loner with morals, ethics and attitudes very different from town-bred tame men like the others about him. Sure, Quint could tame a town and keep it that way. But he still wasn't law. He was a loner and a gunfighter and maybe even something bigger . . . but never law. And sooner or later every town that wanted to survive and prosper had to embrace that law with all its virtues and defects, and stop relying upon substitutes.

They eventually took a vote and it was Rick's own suggestion that when they fired Quint they post him beyond the city limits as well.

They were stunned. Surely it wasn't necessary to go that far? Sack the man then insult him?

Rick insisted, tried to explain. Quint was a loner with a code of his own which would eventually see him clash with those who hired him. No doubt he would be enraged by his sacking and posting, but finally he would go because he would be too proud to stay.

Rick was convincing, and the final decision of the Citizens' Committee of Bonito agreed with him. Posting was the only way. In a tense atmosphere, Chad Stanley put it to the vote. The result was unanimous. Quint Dannecker was to be paid off, sincerely thanked for his services – then posted beyond the town limits of Bonito.

Rick had hoped to locate Quint at the law office but found only a drowsy Mike Tollis there, keeping one sorry boozehound company in the night.

'Reckon he could be over to the High Pocket, Deputy,' Tollis speculated. 'Ain't sighted him since eight or thereabouts . . . it's done gone eleven o'clock now.'

On the street again Rick reckoned it was probably better this way. He'd wanted to keep it private, with just him and Quint having a man-to-man discussion, reaching an amicable agreement and maybe even sharing a drink afterwards. Now he convinced himself it would work better out in the open, such as at the High Pocket bar. After all, this was not a private thing between two men who happened to be brothers. This was about business that would affect the whole town.

He went down the steps and headed along Apache Street for the saloon.

The High Pocket was crowded and noisy as he went through the batwings and halted just inside. Faro and Keno were doing business but not as much as was taking place at the long bar.

He sighted Quint.

He was standing with his back to the west wall at the far end of the bar, hatless and with his head thrown back and laughing. About him were assembled the regular bunch of hunters and punchers and mountain men with whom he liked to associate. Even though Rick had geared himself up for the task before him, he now felt the clammy touch of uncertainty as he studied his brother and fully realized what it was he must do.

That walk across to the bar was as long as any he'd ever taken. Quint welcomed him boisterously and proffered a drink. Rick shook his head. Not tonight. 'I'm here on duty, Quint.'

'Ahhh!' There was a wealth of implication in that breathy sigh, and in the next moment, Quint was eyeing him suspiciously as he said, 'You been to that committee meeting?'

'That's right. It was about you mostly.'

Quint studied his glass. 'They vote to fire me?'

'No. They voted me to post you out of Bonito.'

There it was. Out. He saw flame flicker in his brother's green eyes. It seemed the saloon had hushed, as though every man present sensed what was taking place.

'I'm dead sorry, Quint, but that's how it's got to be.'

Quint toyed with his glass, seemingly for an eternity. 'So, you are running me out of town, Rick boy?'

'Hell, Quint . . . it's not like that. You—'

'Nobody tells me to move on. Not ever.'

This was a Quint he barely knew. He felt his face redden. 'I'll give you until daylight. After that I'd have to come after you.'

'Bring your gun.'

'I-I guess I will.'

Quint raised his glass and their eyes met. 'Well, then, see you come morning time.'

'Yeah, morning time.'

Rick turned and left quickly through the silent, staring ranks. The cold air of the street struck like a blow, causing his injured hand to ache.

He made his way slowly along Apache Street, holding himself tightly like a clenched fist. The five-pointed star pinned to his vest seemed to weigh like lead over his heart.

It was the hour before dawn as Rick came like a sleep-walker along the echoing planks of the boardwalk . . . along the empty white street.

Down along Sullivan Street he could barely make out the ugly bulk of the Golden Hind Hotel, lightless and asleep. A few stars still showed, but most were gone. He passed by the Cattlemen's Association building and the empty rocking chairs along the veranda of Appleseed Hotel and felt a strange sense of ownership of this vacant town in the early morning.

Then it was across Aspen Street and beyond the Bonito Bank, the Green Dollar Café, the Bonito Fast Freight Company and the General Store.

His town.

He unlocked the heavy front door of the jailhouse and let himself in. Tossing the keyring on the table, he went through in back. It was deserted. He had released one drunk and sent turnkey Mike Tollis home at midnight. The office had the familiar smell of stone and timber, the pungent scent of lime and the subtle smell of gun-oil.

He lit a lamp and held his hands briefly over the flame for the warmth. It was a sharp morning and there had been no heating over in O'Leary's Barn where he'd spent the night in the hayloft. No heating – and no father, brother, best pard or lover to try to talk him out of what he must do.

Shaking his head he flexed the fingers of his right hand. There was some stiffness yet he knew it could still draw and shoot a gun – if he must.

He stripped off his shirt and scrubbed his flesh with a swab dipped in icy water from a crockery pitcher. He went to his locker and took out a clean shirt. He put it on with care then spent several minutes working polish into his calf boots. He donned his leather vest and attached the deputy's star after rubbing it to a shine.

He paused for a moment, lost in thought, before buckling on the gunbelt, cinching it in a notch tighter than usual to ease that crawling chill in his belly which he couldn't deny.

Then he produced a rum bottle half-full of oil, and a rag, and sat at the table to clean the Colt and wipe it dry. He repeated this process until the .45 calibre shone dully in the lamplight. He replaced the cartridges in the cylinder, lowered the hammer down upon the single empty chamber, then seated the Colt in its holster and scrubbed the oil from his hands.

He was ready.

He went out into the street as the first thin rays of the sun filtered along Apache Street. He stood on the jailhouse porch with his arms hanging loosely at his sides. Pale faces had already shown at several windows and many a porch chair was filled upon the porches of the Appleseed, the High Pocket and the New York Café with eager spectators.

The dust of the street showed cleanly white and the breeze from the east was fresh against his face and still chill. He felt the weight of a hundred eyes, pitying, speculative, confused and some admiring. Down by the bank he picked out Chad Stanley and knew the slight figure at his side to be Judy.

Lige was there also – come to witness the horror of son against son. Quint appeared around the corner of the New York Café.

He was mounted on the big black, leaning backwards a little in the saddle with feet thrust well forward in the stirrups. Man and mount both stood out sharply in the first bars of yellow sunlight which glinted on bridle buckles and conchos and caressed the Mexican silverwork on the big Texas-Spanish saddle.

Rick stepped down into the street and walked south towards the oncoming horseman. He moved neither fast nor slow, holding his head level, dimly aware that he felt no reality. He could see the slant of Quint's shell belt clear through the opening of his unbuttoned leather jacket and the dull shine of the silver-chased Navy Colt.

From the corner of his eye he watched Judy as he passed the bank. His father was with her and their eyes were upon him – not Quint. He attempted to nod reassuringly but his neck was stiff, and quickly his eyes turned ahead once more.

Fifty feet separating them . . . twenty-five. Quint looming up before him now atop that huge mount. His wrist brushed gun handle, sending a strange shock along his arm. He halted with feet apart and the big black horse in turn drew up before him.

He cleared his throat. 'I gave you until dawn to get out of town.'

'So you did, Rick, so you did.'

'It's dawn now.'

Quint shifted in the saddle to gaze all around – at the street, the sky and the folks along the plankwalks as if seeing for himself whether this was or was not a fact. It seemed a long moment before he again looked down at Rick with a lazy grin – and reached towards his gun!

The shocked sound of the mob in his ears, Rick grabbed for his weapon, expecting at every moment to feel the smash of the killing shot exploding in his body. But with his weapon half-clear, he suddenly froze. For Quint's lethal hands were not filled with a storming Colt, they were instead unbuckling his shell belt.

Rick's gaze snapped up to his brother's face in disbelief. Quint just smiled that lazy, familiar smile and went on removing the belt. He stripped it from his hips and held it forward, the beautifully cared-for weapon still secure in its holster.

'You've earned this,' he said softly. 'It's yours.'

'But—' Rick's voice sounded strange to his own ears. 'I don't understand. . . .'

'I'm not sure I do either, brother. C'mon. Take it before I change my mind.'

Rick allowed his own Colt to slip back into the holster. He reached up and took the proffered gunrig, surprised by its heavyiness. Quint casually rested his hands upon the saddle horn and gazed around Apache Street. His manner was non-chalant yet Rick saw his eyes were sharp and bright, as if he were storing up this picture of the town for some future time when he might recall it to mind.

He then spoke slowly: 'You've got a nice little cow-town here, Rick boy. I figure it'll be a city one day – with big high buildings and women in Paris hats. Yeah, it'll be a big town . . . is a big town in some ways already. Guess it sure must be something special for a man to be ready to die for it.'

He smiled then, that wide, reckless smile that Rick had always remembered before he'd come back, even when the face and form were all near forgotten. 'You keep it this way, boy – your way. Could well be that maybe that's the best way there is.'

He tipped his hat and kneed the black forward. Rick stood staring, watching him move off with Quint's ornate gunrig draped over his arm.

'Quint!'

But Quint didn't turn, didn't pause. He halted just once on the way in front of the bank to salute the grey old man in the chair and then let the black dance away, small puffs of white dust lifting from its hoofs.

'Rick!'

Judy came flying from the porch, hair and skirt billowing behind her. She didn't stop until she was in his arms, murmuring incomprehensible things against his chest. He smiled at her distantly and they turned together to watch the receding rider on the tall black horse slowly merge with the morning mist rising out along the river trail.

On the porch of the bank, Chad Stanley's voice carried clearly to everyone within earshot. 'Well, I don't reckon there'll be any argument as to who our very first sheriff will be.'

This was welcomed with shouts of approval along the street but it was doubtful if the young couple walking off down Apache Street together heard a word. But they smiled and Judy slipped her arm through Rick's – the arm that still had that flashy gunrig looped through it. Together they passed the general store, the Bonito Fast Freight and the Green Dollar Café.

Rick paused to glance up at the flagpole and the half-mast flag. He made a mental note to have them repair that worn rope. A thing like that could make a town look untidy.